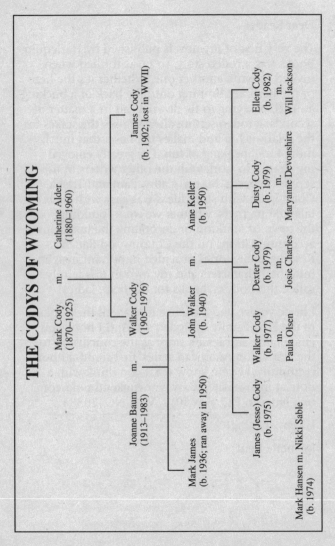

THE CODYS OF WYOMING

Mark Cody (1870–1925) m. Catherine Alder (1880–1960)

James Cody (b. 1902; lost in WWII)

Walker Cody (1905–1976) m. Joanne Baum (1913–1983)

Mark James (b. 1936; ran away in 1950)

John Walker (b. 1940) m. Anne Keller (b. 1950)

James (Jesse) Cody (b. 1975)

Walker Cody (b. 1977) m. Paula Olsen

Dexter Cody (b. 1979) m. Josie Charles

Dusty Cody (b. 1979) m. Maryanne Devonshire

Ellen Cody (b. 1982) m. Will Jackson

Mark Hansen m. Nikki Sable (b. 1974)

Dear Reader,

The very first of my novels published by Harlequin Books was a rodeo story, so I was thrilled when invited to write another one. Whether it's the hero or the heroine climbing onto the back of a bucking animal, or trying to tie down a calf in a matter of seconds, a rodeo setting always raises the stakes for the relationship and makes the book that much more fun. Speaking of fun, I've greatly enjoyed my chance to work with the other writers in this series—Rebecca, Marin, Cathy, Pam and Trisha. Coming up with story ideas was easy with such talented partners, whether we were "building" the town of Markton or decorating the luxurious accommodations on the Cottonwood Ranch. Reading their stories provided important insights into their characters and my own in this family called the Codys. Thanks for the help, ladies!

I hope you've had a chance to read all the books in the First Family of Rodeo set. And I hope you enjoy Janie and Jesse's story as the conclusion to the Harlequin American series' first multi-author continuity. Let me know what you think with a note at my website, www.lynnettekentbooks.com, or a letter to P.O. Box 1012, Vass, NC, 28384.

Happy reading!

Lynnette Kent

Jesse:
Merry Christmas,
Cowboy

LYNNETTE KENT

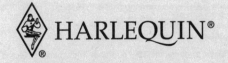

TORONTO • NEW YORK • LONDON
AMSTERDAM • PARIS • SYDNEY • HAMBURG
STOCKHOLM • ATHENS • TOKYO • MILAN • MADRID
PRAGUE • WARSAW • BUDAPEST • AUCKLAND

Recycling programs
for this product may
not exist in your area.

ISBN-13: 978-0-373-75334-5

JESSE: MERRY CHRISTMAS, COWBOY

www.eHarlequin.com

Printed in U.S.A.

ABOUT THE AUTHOR

Lynnette Kent lives on a farm in southeastern North Carolina with her five horses and five dogs. When she isn't busy riding, driving or feeding animals, she loves to tend her gardens and read and write books. This is her twenty-fourth story for Harlequin Books.

Books by Lynnette Kent

HARLEQUIN AMERICAN ROMANCE

1187—CHRISTMAS AT BLUE MOON RANCH
1217—SMOKY MOUNTAIN REUNION
1227—SMOKY MOUNTAIN HOME
1284—A HOLIDAY TO REMEMBER

HARLEQUIN SUPERROMANCE

824—WHAT A MAN'S GOT TO DO
868—EXPECTING THE BEST
901—LUKE'S DAUGHTERS
938—MATT'S FAMILY
988—NOW THAT YOU'RE HERE
1002—MARRIED IN MONTANA
1024—SHENANDOAH CHRISTMAS
1080—THE THIRD MRS. MITCHELL*
1118—THE BALLAD OF DIXON BELL*
1147—THE LAST HONEST MAN*
1177—THE FAKE HUSBAND*
1229—SINGLE WITH KIDS*
1245—ABBY'S CHRISTMAS*
1326—THE PRODIGAL TEXAN

*At the Carolina Diner

Don't miss any of our special offers. Write to us at the following address for information on our newest releases.

Harlequin Reader Service
U.S.: 3010 Walden Ave., P.O. Box 1325, Buffalo, NY 14269
Canadian: P.O. Box 609, Fort Erie, Ont. L2A 5X3

For the man who taught me
what to expect from heroes…my dad.

Chapter One

Ten days. Ten go-rounds. One National Finals Rodeo Championship.

Jesse Cody needed to stay focused on his training in order to win the bull-riding championship. He *didn't* need this.

"Please," he said, staring at his father, who glared right back at him. "Tell me I didn't just hear what I think I heard."

His mother responded, instead. "We invited the Hansens to stay with us at the hotel. Your dad and I will be arriving on Wednesday. But we told Janie you would fly her and Abigail to Las Vegas Tuesday afternoon."

Jesse disconnected from J. W. Cody's flinty gaze and turned to face his mom. "Are we one big, happy family now? Kind of sudden, isn't it?"

"It's taken thirty damn years," J.W. growled.

"We have to adjust, son." Anne Cody put her hand on Jesse's arm and looked up into his face. "Mark Hansen is your father's son. I think the best way to deal with the situation is to accept the facts and move on."

"I—" Jesse shook his head and tried again. "We—" Speechless with frustration, he stepped away from his mom's touch and walked to the wall of windows in his dad's office, which looked out across the sprawling Cottonwood Ranch. Winter had descended on Wyoming, bleaching the prairie grass, defrocking the cottonwood trees of every last leaf and sending the tender plants in the gardens around his parents' house deep underground. The Thanksgiving holiday had ended and Christmas was just around the corner.

The holidays would come after the National Finals, of course, where he fully expected to win the championship in bull riding. That would mean defeating Mark Hansen, his archrival since they were in high school and, it seemed, his older brother. His bastard older brother.

Without turning around, he said, "I don't think Mark and I can live practically on top of each other while we're competing at the Finals."

Again, his mother answered. "You don't spend that much time in the room. I doubt you'll see each other."

"The Hansens actually accepted this invitation?"

"Your father and I had a long talk with Mark and Nicki at the Denver rodeo this past weekend, and they agreed this would be the best solution."

"I bet they did." Who wouldn't want to trade some cheap motel on the Vegas strip for rooms on the concierge floor at a first-class resort? Jesse wasn't surprised that Mark would agree to everything he could get out of becoming a Cody, but his wife, Nicki, had been Jesse's best friend since they were kids. Marrying Hansen had apparently put her solidly on the other side.

His tone of voice must have hinted at his thoughts. "Don't jump to conclusions, Jesse." His mother walked up behind him, took hold of his shoulder and urged him to face her. "As things stood, Janie would have had to stay home to take care of their mother. This way, we can hire a caretaker to keep an eye on Abigail while Janie gets to have fun and watch the Finals. You know she'll want to see Elly race."

"Not to mention Mark," Jesse pointed out. "She'll be rooting for him to win."

Anne grinned. "She can't always be right."

The best Jesse could do in reply was a snort. He looked over at his dad. "And you're okay with this plan? You're ready to welcome Mark into the fold?"

J.W. stuck out his chin. "I think I owe him the recognition."

"What else do you owe him, do you think? A job here at the ranch? In the cattle operation, maybe?"

"We haven't talked about it."

Temper rumbled through Jesse's gut. "I've been running things for eight years. Maybe you think it's time for a change."

"Jesse," his mother said, a warning note in her voice.

"That's bull." J.W. stepped out from behind his desk. "And you know it."

"And maybe you think he needs a spread of his own, to make up for all the years you ignored him. Would a hundred thousand acres do it? Not leased land, of course—just some prime Cottonwood property. Then you could build him and Nicki a house of their own."

"You're acting like a spoiled brat." J.W. moved in close until his nose almost touched Jesse's. "You've had everything you wanted or needed for your whole life. Don't begrudge my son a little attention, maybe some help getting started in life."

Jesse shrugged. "Of course not. You're free to give him whatever makes you feel better, Dad. Even though Hansen hasn't worked a single day on this land, never squeezed out a single drop of sweat."

"None of you kids has—"

"Now who's talking bull?" Hands propped on his hips, Jesse moved forward a step. His father retreated. "I've been working on this ranch since I was old enough to sit a horse. You've been ordering me around, telling me what I had to do, had to know, where I should be and how I should think for as long as I remember. There hasn't been a day I didn't feel responsible for every damn problem and solution going on at the Cottonwood Ranch. So don't tell me I haven't worked for what I got."

He did a quick turn on his heel and headed for the door.

"You don't walk out of here without my permission."

Jesse heard his mother's gasp as he stopped in his tracks. He stared at the closed door panel for a few seconds, debating what to say.

Then, without another word, he reached for the knob, pushed through the door and strode across the foyer, past the life-size sculpture of a cowboy on his horse, to the front entrance. Another minute and he was in his truck, headed down the road at a reckless speed. He braked briefly underneath the wrought-iron sign announcing The Cottonwood Ranch, glanced in both directions and jerked the steering wheel left. Once on the paved county road, he pushed hard on the gas pedal, letting the big diesel engine whine.

He wanted a good stiff drink…or four or five, however many shots it took to shut down his brain. And he wanted to drink alone, though not in private. Drinking behind closed doors only led to trouble.

But he couldn't think of anywhere in the whole state of Wyoming where he would be anonymous. Not in the closest little town, Markton, or even in Cody, a few miles farther on. Not in Laramie or Cheyenne or Gillette, where he had friends and knew competitors. He was an NFR finalist in bull riding, after all. Worse, he was a Cody—J. W. Cody's *second* son. Not much happened to the Codys that didn't become public knowledge.

And that was as good a reason for hard drinking as Jesse had ever come up with.

AFTER WORKING A FULL DAY at the Markton Feed and Grain Store, Janie still had errands to run if she planned to leave for Las Vegas tomorrow. In Jesse Cody's plane.

That thought alone made her stumble as she walked across the pharmacy parking lot with her four bags of supplies. Or maybe hunger tripped her up—she hadn't eaten since breakfast and her stomach had been growling for hours. If she planned to keep shopping, she should probably get some food.

Back in her truck, grateful to be out of the bitter wind blowing off the mountains, she headed for her favorite restaurant in Cody. Managed by a couple of her friends from Markton, Los Potrillos served well-cooked, authentic Mexican food. A quick bite would give her the energy she needed to spend the rest of the night packing her mother's bag as well as her own for the trip to Las Vegas.

Janie still didn't see how this trip could possibly succeed. Who in their right mind would take an Alzheimer's patient traveling? These days, her mother left their house only for doctors' appointments, and then spent the entire trip agitated and fearful. What would she think about an airplane flight? How would she react in a small private jet?

And what in the world would Janie find to talk about

with Jesse Cody for two solid hours? Especially when the most obvious topic—the fact that her brother Mark was also his brother—was too fraught with tension to discuss?

With her hands clenched on the steering wheel, she pulled into a parking spot at the restaurant, then kept her head down against the wind-driven sleet as she ran inside.

"Lousy weather," her friend Lila remarked, leading her to a booth for two.

"Nasty," Janie agreed, brushing ice crystals off her shoulders. "Some good hot food will help, though."

Lila smiled. "You know we've got that covered."

The waitress appeared to take Janie's order for coffee, water and chicken mole. Not many people had ventured out on a Monday night in bad weather, and the dining room tables were mostly empty. Janie wished she were home, too, eating canned tomato soup in front of the TV instead of planning to hit the superstore in Cody to find clothes for her mom to wear in Vegas.

Her mom…the woman who had tempted J. W. Cody into an adulterous affair.

Janie couldn't stifle a sigh. If she'd ever had the ghost of a chance with Jesse, she felt sure that chance had now vaporized. Whenever he looked at her, he would be reminded of her brother…okay, her half brother, but still…Mark's new status as a Cody threatened everything Jesse had worked for in his life—the respect of folks in town and across the country as J. W. Cody's oldest son, his place in the business at the Cottonwood Ranch and maybe even the title of World Champion Bull Rider at the National Finals Rodeo.

"Here you go." The waitress set a huge platter of

chicken with chocolate sauce, salad and tortillas on the table in front of her.

"Thanks." Janie flashed a smile, even though her appetite had all but vanished. Thinking too much about Jesse Cody always made her want to curl up into a ball and cry her eyes out.

As the server headed toward the kitchen in the back of the building, somewhere behind Janie a man called out, loudly enough to be heard over the music.

"Excuse me?"

With a fork full of mole halfway to her mouth, Janie groaned. Could she be this unlucky? As if her thoughts had conjured him, Jesse Cody sat at a table in the back.

"Excuse me," he said again when the waitress didn't turn.

Sauce dripped onto Janie's plate. She squeezed her eyes shut, willing him not to notice her.

Boot heels thudded on the tile floor, coming up beside her table. He passed, and Janie opened her eyes.

Broad-shouldered and slim-hipped, his short, silvery-blond hair gleaming even in the dim lighting, Jesse walked away from her, carrying an empty highball glass toward the bar. As she watched, he thumped the tumbler down on the counter. For years, she'd been imagining the strength of his muscle-corded arms around her, the rumble of his warm, smooth voice against her heart. Now, she shook her head. *As if!*

"Could I get a refill, please? Jack on the rocks. Make it a double this time."

He would turn back in a minute. She couldn't avoid being seen.

With the precision of a surgeon, Janie returned her untouched food to the plate. She took a gulp of water and wiped her mouth. Then she folded her hands in her lap and put a smile on her face—a friendly, casual smile, she hoped—that said, "Don't let me keep you."

Jesse took a sip from his new drink while still standing at the bar. Then he pivoted and started back to his table. Janie witnessed the moment he caught sight of her, saw the surprise in his blue eyes, quickly followed by irritation, outright anger and then resignation. Just as she'd expected.

Her heart sank. She thought she might be sick.

To give the man credit, the negative reaction lasted only a second, replaced by his usual engaging grin. "Hi, Janie." His jovial tone suggested they were good friends. "What brings you to Cody for dinner?" He glanced at the empty seat across from her. "All alone?"

"Hey, Jesse." Her fingers curled into fists under the table. "Yeah, just a quick bite. I had some last-minute shopping."

He glanced toward the table behind her, then back at the empty seat in her booth. "I can keep you company a little while, if you'd like."

"Sure." As he sat down, Janie wondered how she would manage to swallow a single bite. "You're here by yourself?" Without meaning to, she looked down at the glass between his fingertips.

"Uh, yeah." Even as she watched, he took a long draw on the whiskey. "I had a…discussion…with the parents, and needed to loosen up a little afterward."

Janie could imagine exactly what was discussed. "That's how it goes sometimes." Then she thought about her own mother, no longer capable of ordinary family squabbles or any real relationships. "On the other hand, you miss them when they're…not here anymore."

Looking back at her plate, she picked up her fork

again, put the food in her mouth and chewed, even swallowed without gagging. When she lifted her chin, she found Jesse's gaze fixed on her face.

"Sorry," he said. "I guess we don't always appreciate what we've got till it's gone. How's your mom doing?"

She couldn't tell him the worst parts, not when they were supposed to spend a week in the same hotel. "Okay, I guess. She doesn't remember much. And she sleeps a lot." Maybe that would calm some of his fears about the upcoming trip.

Janie only hoped she was telling the truth.

"I, um, thought we'd leave about two, tomorrow afternoon." Jesse avoided her eyes as he spoke. "Will that work for you?"

She stared at him as he swirled the ice cubes around in his glass. Shadows rimmed his eyes, like bruises from a fist. Now that she considered, he looked like he hadn't slept in days. But she couldn't ask why not. "Shall we meet you at your airstrip?"

Jesse kept his plane on the ranch, taking off and landing on the Codys' private runway. That kind of luxury made it possible for him to compete in the biggest rodeos around the country in order to earn the points and money required to reach the National Finals while being home during the week to work at the ranch. Mark, on the other hand, drove almost everywhere and competed constantly, which meant he was away from home most of the time.

Just one more example of the huge lifestyle gap between the rich Codys and the poor Hansens.

"Why don't I pick you up about one-thirty," Jesse suggested. "You'll need some help with luggage and… and stuff."

She wasn't sure if that would be better or worse than

having her mother see him for the first time at the plane. "That sounds good. Thanks."

Silence fell, then stretched between them because, really, what did they have to say? Janie couldn't tell him what she felt, and as far as Jesse was concerned, she was his little sister's buddy. Or else the sister of his archrival. He could take his pick.

"I'm sorry," she said abruptly. "I know this must be hell for you."

His sigh seemed to come up from the soles of his boots. "It's not easy for anybody."

"Mark is a good man." For some reason she needed to say that. "He won't hurt your parents if he can help it."

"So Nicki tells me." Jesse gave a faint grin then glanced at her plate. "You're not eating."

"I'm not hungry." She pushed the plate toward him. "Have some."

He didn't wait for a second invitation, but picked up the salad fork she hadn't used and dug in. From the way he ate, she might have concluded he hadn't had a decent meal in months. Judging by the loose fit of his jeans, she might be right.

The waitress stopped by to see if they needed anything, and Jesse ordered another double.

"Don't worry," he said when Janie frowned. "I won't have anything to drink after midnight. Eight hours is the FAA rule for private pilots, same as the airlines."

"What about the drive home?" A glance through the window showed the sleet had turned to snow which already coated the roads.

"I can drive from Cody to Markton in my sleep." He drained the dregs of one glass just as the server set down the new one. "And probably have, about a hundred times. If not more."

"I believe you. That doesn't make it safe to drive drunk."

"It's okay." His words slurred a little. "I'm just another one of those intre…interchangeable younger Cody brothers. Mark's got the hard job now. To Mark." He raised his glass. "The old man's pride 'n' joy. His new pride 'n' joy, that is." Half the whiskey vanished with his first gulp. Jesse swallowed and then emptied the drink.

"That's a stupid thing to say." Janie gripped the edge of the table with her fingertips. "Walker and Dusty and Dex have never been jealous of you. You don't deserve a pity party any more than they do."

"You know so much." He slid out of the booth, swaying a little as he straightened up. "S'hard to miss what you never had."

"Mark isn't taking anything away from you. He just wants—"

"To know his dad, right?" Stepping carefully, he retrieved his jacket and hat from the other table, then came back to stand beside her again. "He'll find out soon enough that being J. W. Cody's oldest son comes with a price. I hope your brother's man enough to pay it."

The implied insult stung. "Why wouldn't he be? He's as much a Cody as you are."

In the process of thumbing through his wallet for cash, Jesse stilled. After a moment, he lifted his gaze to her face.

"That's the truth, isn't it? I've got no more claim on J.W. than your brother does, except for a marriage license that didn't seem to mean too much at the time."

He tossed a couple of bills on the table, an amount that would cover his drinks plus the dinner she hadn't eaten twice over. "So maybe it's my turn to get out from under the Cody yoke. Your brother—"

"Your brother," Janie interrupted.

"Mark," he growled, "can have all the honors. Hell, maybe he'll just go on and take the championship while he's at it." He jammed his white hat on his head and shrugged into his heavy sheepskin coat. "I don't really give a damn about anything or anybody. Not any-more."

And with that declaration, Jesse Cody turned on his heel and stalked out into the snowy night.

Chapter Two

The frigid wind hit Jesse like a brick in the face. He staggered, eyes narrowed against the prick of icy snow pellets.

"Hell of a night for a drive," he muttered, heading for his truck.

Once inside the cab, he wiped snowflakes off his face, fired up the engine and flipped the heater fan to high speed, then took off his hat and let his head rest back against the seat. Maybe if he closed his eyes, he'd fall asleep. This wouldn't be the first parking lot where he'd stopped to grab a few winks before a long drive.

Might be one of the last, though. He was getting too old for bull riding, too old for the whole damn rodeo lifestyle. Even with a plane to get him to shows across the country, the endless competitions wore him out. The fact that Mark Hansen had hit enough shows and earned enough money to reach the Finals by driving from one venue to the next made him a damn good cowboy. He probably deserved to win the championship based on endurance alone.

Nobody could deny the man's talent, either. Hansen made sitting astride a two-thousand pound package of bovine dynamite look like a pony ride at the county fair.

Yawning, eyelids drooping, Jesse dragged his brain away from the possibility that anyone but a Cody—all right, this Cody—would win the championship. He visualized the scene on the final night at the Thomas & Mack Center, pictured himself on stage accepting the winner's saddle, the belt buckle…his dad would have to be proud of him then…

In his dream, the indoor arena stage in Vegas became a simple outdoor platform under the hot Texas sun. "Ladies and gentlemen," blasted a voice out of the loudspeaker. "This afternoon's winner in the junior bull-riding division is…Mr. Mark Hansen!"

Jesse watched, gut churning, as a whip-thin teenaged Mark stepped up to claim the belt buckle and a check.

Standing at Jesse's shoulder, his dad muttered, "Hansen's got the talent, no doubt about it. You should have that kind of split-second timing. God knows you're as much a Cody—" The words stopped abruptly.

Jesse didn't look around when, after a couple of seconds, his dad finished the thought. "As your brothers, and they all got it. You need to work harder, is all. Practice more."

Applause and cheers chased Jesse as he broke away and fought through the crowd, looking for an exit…

The sharp rap of knuckles on the window right beside his head woke him up. Jesse snorted and jumped, then swore as he fumbled for the window button. The glass slid down and a thick layer of snow fell onto his lap.

"Dammit." He brushed the snow away, glaring at the woman peering in at him. She'd pulled the hood of her parka over her hair, leaving only her dark eyes and rosy mouth and smooth cheeks vulnerable to the wind and cold. "What the hell do you want, Janie?"

His temper didn't faze her. "I thought you might have passed out here in the parking lot."

"After three drinks?" Jesse snorted. "Come on."

"You've been sitting there for two hours. I went shopping and came back and you're still here."

"Nah." He glanced at the clock on the dash. Two hours had, in fact, passed since he got into the truck. "Oh. Well, I dozed off. It's been a long day. I was in the saddle at 6:00 a.m."

"So you should be at home asleep."

"Great. Let me roll up the window and I'll go do that."

Janie shook her head. "Why don't you move to the passenger side and let me drive you home?"

"I don't think so." Hearing his own surliness, Jesse shook his head and tried for some good manners. "I appreciate the concern, really, but I'm fine. Take yourself back to Markton and I'll see you tomorrow."

The woman appeared to be deaf. She reached through the open window, pulled up the handle and opened the door. "Come on, Jesse. Better safe than sorry."

He didn't intend to budge. "You're talking to a bull rider, here. I don't do safe."

"Yeah, a bull rider who is supposed to compete at the world championships starting on Thursday night. Wouldn't you like to be alive for the event?"

He groaned in frustration. "I am not drunk."

"You're tired. That's enough of an excuse."

"What about your truck?"

"Roberto and Lila said they'd bring it home for me tonight when they close. Come on, Jesse." She rubbed her gloved hands over her arms. "It's freezing out here."

They could argue all night, or he could give in just to get some peace. "I don't know why I'm letting you do this." He dropped to the pavement, keeping his balance by gripping the door, since the ground seemed a little unsteady under his feet. "It's absurd. I'm stone-cold sober."

"Sure you are." Janie turned to the small, beat-up truck parked next to his and opened the door. "Put these in the backseat." A dozen or so shopping bags came at him with the order. Once the goods were stowed, she climbed up behind the steering wheel without looking at him until she'd shut the door between them. "Coming?"

If only to get out of the snow, Jesse rounded the truck bed to the passenger side and swung himself onto the seat, remembering just in time to move his hat. With his safety belt buckled, he sat staring out the window as Janie Hansen, his designated driver, took him home.

Snow powdered the windshield as the streetlights of Cody dimmed behind them on the dark road to Markton. Several inches of the white stuff covered the road pavement, while twice that much had already piled up on the frozen grass.

The storm intensified, and Janie slowed down as visibility decreased. "Are we going to be able to take off tomorrow?" she asked. "If the sky clears, I mean."

"We can plow the runway." Jesse rubbed his sleepy eyes with his fingers. "And the plane's in the hangar, so there won't be ice on the wings. Don't worry," he said, noticing how her teeth bit at her full lower lip. "I'll keep you and your mom safe."

She answered with a sigh, which hinted at trouble.

He decided he'd better know what lay ahead. "Is your mom looking forward to the trip?" When Janie didn't answer, he pushed. "Does she know what's going on?"

"Sometimes," Janie said at last. "She wants to watch Mark in the Finals. When she remembers."

"You've told her about the flight?"

She sent him a worried glance. "I tried to."

"How do you think she'll react?"

He heard the gulp as she swallowed hard. "I have no idea."

"Great." He couldn't repress the comment and wouldn't apologize. "If you didn't think this was going to work, why did you agree to come?"

She stared straight ahead, lips pressed together, for a long time. Her whitened knuckles revealed a tense grip on the steering wheel. "Mark and Nicki wanted Mom to come. Anyway, how many times have you refused to do what your parents wanted?"

Good point. "You've got an advantage over the rest of us, though."

"Oh?"

"You're not part of the family."

"No kidding?"

The sarcasm stung. "You don't have to get mad. I just meant—"

She held up a hand to stop him. "Believe me, I know exactly how far outside the Cody constellation my family's orbit lies."

Jesse let the comment slide. "I only meant that my parents don't have any power over you. You were free to refuse."

"And miss maybe the only time I'll ever get to see my brother at the National Finals? Maybe the only time I ever get to go to the Finals, period?" She shook her head. "I couldn't say no."

"I guess you couldn't." He would just have to hope things turned out better than he expected.

Several miles passed in a silence broken only by the sound of the wipers brushing back and forth. Finally, Jesse came up with a less confrontational topic. "So you've never been to the Finals?"

"Nope."

"It's the wildest rodeo you can imagine. Picture any show you've ever been to times a thousand, held in the craziest place on the planet."

Janie chuckled. "That's quite a description. But this is your first time competing, too. Right?"

"Yeah. We go every year since Dad usually has a bull competing, but I was tired of hearing him complain that I wasn't there riding, so I put in the extra effort and got myself on the list." He winced when he recognized the bitterness in his own voice. "Of course, I'm looking forward to competing. The best bulls and the best riders—it's gonna be a blast."

He felt Janie's sideways appraisal. "Are you ready for all the attention that comes with the title? I'm pretty sure Mark hasn't thought about it at all."

"Endorsements, you mean? And publicity?" She nodded. "I don't think any of the guys thinks about that ahead of time. We all just want to get out there and win. That's the real point—being the best."

"Till next year. Or maybe just the next ride."

"Whoa. Don't be so supportive."

She shrugged, then made a careful turn onto the road leading between stone pillars into the Cottonwood Ranch. "I like winning as much as anybody. If Mark gets the championship, I know he'll spend some of the money to help take care of Mom, which will be a blessing. But you don't need the cash, or the fame. I get the feeling that even if you win, you won't be satisfied."

Jesse turned in his seat to look across the cab at

her. "What else could I want? Besides being world champion?"

As he asked the question, Janie braked gently at the foot of the porch steps leading to his front door. "I think you want respect." She didn't look at him as she answered but watched as a layer of snow quickly obscured her view through the windshield.

The woman knew too damn much about what went on inside his head. "Who doesn't?"

Then her eyes met his. "The man who already respects himself."

Stunned by the implication, Jesse couldn't have come up with a quick, casual answer if his life depended on it. At last he simply opened the door and jumped down into the snow, sinking halfway to his knees. "Maybe this worked out okay, after all," he told Janie, grateful to have something practical to think about. "This way, you can just drive the truck back here tomorrow when you come with your mom."

"Sure." Janie looked past him at the dark windows of the old homestead the Cody siblings used to share. "I guess you're living all by yourself these days, since Dex is with Josie and Elly's with Will."

He nodded. "Most of the time."

"Do you get lonely?"

She'd already divined more secrets tonight than he was comfortable with. "After growing up with the pack of them following me around? I'm enjoying the peace and quiet." He patted the roof of the truck. "I'll see you tomorrow afternoon, about one-thirty. Drive carefully."

"Right. And you be sure to get lots of sleep, so I won't be nervous while we fly tomorrow." Her smile was rueful. "More nervous than I already am, anyway."

His tired brain picked up the hint. "Is this your first time flying?"

Janie nodded. "I'm an aeronautical virgin, so to speak."

He laughed. "I'll be gentle." Stepping back, he shut the door and then called through the glass, "Thanks for the ride home."

"You're welcome." She waved, shifted the truck into four-wheel drive and drove away, leaving Jesse standing outside in the false twilight of a snowy night.

He stood there for quite some time, watching the snow fall while he wondered what else Janie Hansen might know about him that he wished she didn't.

THE FLIGHT TURNED OUT to be easier—and yet more difficult—than Janie could have imagined.

Her mother's doctor had provided a sedative for the trip, and even half a dose kept Abby Hansen too sleepy to get upset about leaving the house in a truck she didn't recognize for a place she didn't know. Janie hated the dull, lifeless expression on her mother's face as they drove the snowy roads toward the Codys' property, but if the alternative was hysteria, she'd take dull.

Once she reached the Cottonwood Ranch, she saw that Jesse had seen to it that the ranch roads were cleared, as well as the runway. That would be the advantage of having a crew of cowboys ready to take whatever orders came into the boss's head. She reached the runway without a problem, having ridden the land on horseback for years with Elly, Jesse's sister. The storm had passed to the east, leaving a cloudless blue sky above the snow-blanketed prairie. Jesse's plane sat there gleaming in the sunlight—ready, Janie gathered, to take off.

She wished she could say the same. Not knowing

what to expect and anticipating looking down from this small craft to the earth thousands of feet below only made her feel sick to her stomach. Maybe she should have taken one of her mom's pills.

Getting her mother onto the plane took her mind off her own anxiety. Abigail had fallen asleep on the ride from town and was startled to be woken up. She didn't recognize Jesse, and his attempts at friendliness didn't reassure her.

"Where is he taking us?" Abby whispered to Janie as they crossed the tarmac toward the plane. "Is he some kind of new doctor?"

"No, Mom. Just a friend. We're going to see Mark at the rodeo, remember?"

"Mark's a good boy. And he's the best bull rider in the world. He's going to win, isn't he?"

They reached the bottom of the steps that led up into the plane. "Yes, he is." Janie glanced back at Jesse and saw his rueful smile. "Let me help you up the steps, okay?"

The passenger cabin reminded Janie of a luxurious motor home she'd seen once at a big rodeo, with reclining armchair seats that swiveled in all directions and an up-to-date TV and music system. The walls were paneled with beautiful wood, thick carpet covered the floor and a small kitchen offered snacks and drinks of all kinds.

The thought that Mark was now part of a family that could afford such luxury made Janie shake her head. What sane person wouldn't choose this lifestyle, given the option?

Abigail didn't like the smallness of the plane, but the sedative made her too tired to do more than talk about her feelings.

"There's not enough room," she said, her voice fretful. "Only a few seats. Where will everyone else sit, Janie?"

"Don't worry, they'll find a place, Mom. Why don't you lean back and let me fasten your seat belt?" By the time she got Abby settled and interested in a travel magazine with lots of photographs, Jesse had climbed aboard, shutting the door behind him.

"Ready?" Underneath the sheepskin coat, he wore the standard rodeo "uniform"—good jeans with one of his trophy belt buckles, dressy boots and a Western shirt in a soft blue chambray that made his eyes an even brighter blue by comparison. Weak-kneed with nerves and longing, Janie sank into the seat beside her mother. "Um…sure." Her hands shook as she buckled her own belt.

Jesse grinned. "You don't sound too sure. I promise, everything will be fine. The weather is great, the plane's in perfect condition, and I am a terrific pilot."

She couldn't resist a little dig. "Modest, too."

"Always. Just relax, and we'll be flying high in no time."

"That's what I'm afraid of," Janie muttered.

She could see him in the pilot's chair from where she sat. He donned a set of earphones, then flipped switches, turned knobs and consulted charts, plus a hundred other complicated motions she guessed were necessary to make the plane function. Finally, with a slight bump, they started rolling along the ground.

Janie looked over at her mother, who was asleep again, her head resting against the butterscotch-colored leather of her seat, the magazine in her lap. Janie realized her own hands now gripped the arm-rests, but just when she thought she might loosen her hold, they hit another bump. Then another. Were they going to die now?

In the next moment, though, the front end of the plane lifted. The noise of wheels on pavement stopped, and she knew they'd taken off. The plane was flying.

She was flying.

A glance out the window showed her the ground falling away, the sky growing larger, enfolding them, supporting them…and then the wonders of a bird's-eye view as they flew southwest, across Yellowstone, the Tetons and Utah. Abby stayed asleep, so before too long, Jesse had lured Janie to the cockpit so they could talk about the wonders she saw beneath the wings.

"I don't want to land," she confessed at last, as they neared Las Vegas and the desert floor came closer. "The magic's in the sky."

Jesse grinned. "Well, we've got to fly back next weekend. Something to look forward to."

Before she could respond, a cry came from the cabin behind them. "Janie? Janie, help me!"

When she reached her mother, Abby grabbed her arm with both hands. "Janie, what's happening? Where am I? What is this place?"

"Shh, Mom. Shh. It's okay." Janie knelt next to her mother's chair, trying to be calm despite the pain of fingernails digging into her arm. "We're going to Las Vegas, remember? Mark's riding in the National Finals and we get to watch. We took an airplane, so we didn't have to drive so far. Remember?"

But Abby didn't remember and Janie spent the rest of the flight trying to reassure her and calm her down, thankful for the seat belt which kept her mother in the chair. Her moans and cries would be easily heard by

Jesse up in the cockpit. The last twenty minutes of the trip approached Janie's worst fears.

Just as her mother had subsided for a moment, Jesse's voice came over the intercom. "Janie, sorry to bother you, but you'll need to be in a seat with a safety belt for the next few minutes while we land."

At the sound of the disembodied voice, Abby became agitated again. With her arm still in her mother's grip, Janie sat in the seat facing Abby's and leaned forward to ease the strain on her shoulder. She couldn't begin to imagine how they would get the hysterical woman off the plane and into a car, much less through a crowded hotel lobby, onto an elevator and settled in a hotel room.

What a terrible idea this had been. Or, rather, how stupid she had been to accept the Codys' invitation. She should have refused and watched Mark ride on TV.

But instead, she'd let Mark and Nicki persuade her to "join the fun." She'd grabbed at the chance to experience the Finals for herself, maybe the only time she'd ever attend the biggest event in professional rodeo.

And maybe the last opportunity she would ever have to make an impression on Jesse Cody. Deep in her heart, unconfessed to anybody else, was the hope that she could maneuver some private time with Jesse. Maybe, if she was really lucky, he might see her as something other than Elly's friend or Mark's sister. She'd certainly shopped for that chance, running up the balance on her credit card way beyond her ability to pay it off any time soon.

Not only had she spent too much money, but she'd dragged her mother away from the home where she felt safe and subjected her to all the terrors of travel. Sure,

Mark's chance at the championship provided an excuse, and he'd wanted Abby to be there.

But Janie knew the truth. If it weren't for her feelings for Jesse, she would have had the strength and good sense to keep her mother at home. How selfish could she be?

With just a couple of slight hops, the plane touched down and claimed the runway surface. Janie barely felt the braking action as Jesse slowed their speed and approached the hangar. Only the smallest jolt signaled that they'd come to a stop.

Jesse appeared in the doorway to the front of the plane, and Abby shrank back into her seat. "Who is that man? What does he want?"

At least she'd finally let go of Janie's arm. "This is Jesse, Mom. He's a f-friend of mine."

Her "friend" came and squatted down by Abby's chair. "I'm going to take you somewhere you'll be safe." He spoke slowly, in the soothing tone Janie had heard him use with frightened horses and puppies. "Would you like that, Abby?" He fixed his wide, steady gaze on hers.

To Janie's surprise, her mother nodded without looking away.

"That's good." His smile was warm and reassuring. Janie could see her mother relax. "We've got a car waiting outside, and then we'll go to a place where you'll feel comfortable."

"I get to go home?"

"Not right away. But Mark is waiting for you. And Janie will be there." Jesse placed a hand over Abby's clenched fingers. "You know Mark and Janie would never let anything happen to you. They will always keep you safe."

Janie smiled through her tears as her mother looked at her.

"I know." Abby nodded. "They take care of me."

Jesse nodded. "I know they do. Now, I'm going to make sure the car is ready and then we'll get in and drive for a little while. Wait for me—I'll be gone just a minute."

When he returned, events proceeded exactly as he'd promised. He coaxed Abby down the steps from the plane and then into a waiting limousine, where he offered her some water and a Snickers bar, her favorite candy. After a short trip, the limousine stopped in the drive of a towering resort building, but the crowds and noise Janie expected were nowhere to be seen.

"The hotel allowed us to use their security entrance," Jesse explained as he helped Janie out of the car. "We'll take the private elevator straight to our floor."

Once he had persuaded her mother out of the limo, Jesse smoothly escorted them both through an empty hallway to an elevator as spacious as most rooms in their home. On the fortieth floor, the doors slid apart and Jesse led them along another wide, silent hallway, this one carpeted in forest-green and decorated with quiet elegance. When he knocked on the door at the very end, they were welcomed by a middle-aged woman with bright silver hair and a deep tan.

"It's good to meet you, Janie. I'm Serena Gable." Her smile and soothing demeanor lived up to her name. Putting an arm around Abby's shoulders, she drew the anxious woman into a large, airy suite of rooms. "Miss Abby, let's get you comfortable."

In minutes, she'd convinced Janie's mother to change into lounge pajamas and crawl between smooth, cool sheets. Her calm voice, with its hint of a Southern accent, and her quiet, efficient movements made Janie feel calmer, too. She was able to kiss her mother on the cheek and leave the bedroom without a single protest being voiced.

"I'll have her awake for dinner," Serena promised as she closed the door.

"Wow." Janie stood in the living room of the suite, bewildered by the sudden absence of responsibility in her life. "That was amazing."

Jesse had waited outside the bedroom while Abby got settled. "I think your mom will be okay while she's here. Don't you?"

"Sure." But the enormity of everything that had happened in the past four hours had finally caught up with Janie. She stared at the man beside her as questions began to pop up in her brain. "How in the world did you arrange all of this?"

"My parents talked to Mark and Nicki, trying to be sure the trip wouldn't be too difficult for your mom."

"Why?"

"What do you mean?"

"Why are they making such an effort?" Janie brushed her bangs off her forehead, then down again. "I mean, your dad hasn't deigned to recognize my mother's existence for more than thirty years. Why start now?"

Jesse's eyes narrowed. "That's kind of a strange question to ask, given that all we're trying to do is be nice to your family."

"Maybe so." With her arms crossed over her chest, Janie lifted her chin. "But smart businessmen like your dad never give away something for nothing. So I want to know what your family expects from the Hansen family in return for all this generosity you're offering."

She gave the matter a second's thought. "Just what is it you're trying to bribe Mark to do?"

Jesse propped his hands on his hips. "I don't—"

"Or are you spending all this money simply to make him leave you alone?"

Chapter Three

Jesse stared at the woman who'd just accused his family of cheating and lying. "You don't mince words, do you?"

"I want to know the truth," she said. "That's all."

At that moment, the bedroom door beside Jesse opened. "Janie?" Mark Hansen looked at his sister, then at Jesse. "I thought that was your voice I heard. What are you two arguing about?" He crossed the living room to Janie and gave her a quick hug. "Tell me how the trip went for Mom."

Jesse took a step back, preparing to turn around and go to his own room.

But Mark motioned him to stay. "Have a seat. Nicki will be here in a minute and she'll be glad to see you."

Jesse hated to admit it, but Nicki's marriage had changed how he felt abut his best friend. He didn't feel comfortable with her these days, not since Mark Hansen had become her husband. "Thanks, but I need to return a few phone calls."

"Okay." Mark assessed him with a keen stare all too similar to J.W.'s. "What did Janie say that's got you worked up?"

"You'll have to ask her. I'll catch up with you all later,

okay?" Without waiting for an answer, Jesse left and headed down the hallway to the suite his parents always reserved for the Finals. In past years, J.W. and Anne had occupied the master bedroom, Elly had taken the room with only one queen-size bed and the four brothers had slept wherever they found space in the remaining bedroom and on various couches.

This year, the other Cody kids were staying in their own rooms with their new partners, leaving Jesse his choice of both secondary bedrooms. Standing in the silent living room he realized that, like everything else about the Cody family, the time they spent together at the Finals this year was going to be very different.

And he didn't like the changes. He wanted his normal family back—his dad as the honest, upfront husband Jesse had always believed he was, his mother as a contented and cherished wife, his brothers and sister as the playmates and allies he'd grown up with.

What he did not appreciate was having a new brother who'd already appropriated his best friend and might very well beat him in the championship and take over his job at the ranch. And he did not appreciate being insulted by a woman he was just trying to be nice to… especially when he couldn't swear that his dad wouldn't pull exactly the kind of trick she accused him of.

J. W. Cody had always been a canny negotiator, capable of wheeling and dealing to get the best advantage for the Cottonwood Ranch. Jesse couldn't think of a single reason to doubt the possibility that J.W. would manipulate his bastard son with gifts and attention to further some purpose of his own. If Jesse asked for the truth, his dad would say whatever suited him at the moment.

So he'd have to ferret out proof of what J.W. planned,

if anything, on his own. Just like he'd had to hire William Jackson, Elly's fiancé, to prove Mark's paternity—all in the name of looking out for the Codys and the Cottonwood Ranch.

Walking into the bedroom Elly used to occupy, Jesse dropped facedown on the bed. Sometimes, protecting the ranch and the family felt like a burden he just couldn't carry another step.

And sometimes, these days, he was tempted to believe that Mark Hansen, always strapped for cash and unaware of his heritage as a Cody, had been the luckier man.

WHEN JANIE TOLD MARK what she'd accused J. W. Cody of, Mark stared at her in much the same way Jesse had. "Why would you think something like that, let alone say it out loud? To Jesse, of all people?"

Nicki's expression conveyed the same disapproval. "The Codys aren't like that, Janie. Especially Jesse. You of all people should know how honest he is."

"Maybe Jesse's being duped, just like the two of you." She felt all the more aggravated because she knew she'd been wrong to bring it up. Sometimes her mouth galloped off before her brain settled fully into the saddle. "J. W. Cody isn't above using Jesse to get what he wants."

"And just what do you think that is?" Mark stood with his arms crossed tightly over his chest, as if the position helped him keep his temper.

"Well…" Janie gathered her thoughts together. "If he's seen by everybody at the National Finals being nice to you—taking care of your mother, paying for me to be here, who knows what else he's got planned—that'll be the story people accept about you and the Codys. Then, back at home, he can cut you off and nobody will believe it wasn't your idea. Or—"

Mark made a chopping motion with one stiff hand. "Cut me off? What does that even mean?"

"He could refuse to see you again. Refuse to give you a job, or anything else you're entitled to as his son."

"What makes you think I want a job from J. W. Cody? Or anything else, except acknowledgment that he's my father?"

"Why would you have accepted this invitation, otherwise?"

Mark's cheeks reddened, and after a quick glance at Nicki, he looked at the carpet between the toes of his boots.

"If you intended to remain independent, then I would think you would have been here on your own, not letting the Codys buy you a fancy room and meals and... whatever."

"We thought it would be polite to accept," Nicki said after a pause. "A gesture of good faith."

"But then you involved Mom. And me. That leaves us indebted to a man we're not at all related to."

Mark lifted his head. "The Codys don't expect to be paid back."

"I'm not talking about money. As Nicki just pointed out, there are other mediums of exchange."

Her brother looked confused.

"Hospitality is a gift," Janie explained. "And it's one I can't possibly give back. So now I'm in the Codys' debt. As are you and Nicki. But at least you could work for him, if you wanted to and he asked. I'll just be at a permanent disadvantage."

After another pause, Mark made a gesture of surrender and sat down on the sofa, bringing Nicki with him. "I still don't completely understand your point. I think, and Nicki does, too—" his wife nodded when he looked at her "—we think the Codys just want to have the family all together, as they do for every National Finals. If there's more to it, I'll deal with that when it comes. But I haven't by any means decided that I want to be part of the Cody operation. Nicki and I haven't really had time to talk about it. We were waiting until after the championship." He curved his arm around Nicki's waist, and from the gentle motion of his hand along his wife's hip, Janie could tell that his thoughts had taken a different direction.

"Fine. Once I've unpacked, I'll apologize to Jesse, and I'll try to keep my suspicions to myself. See you guys later." No one, she noticed, was asking her to stay and keep them company. She didn't turn around to discover why no one answered.

In the bedroom on the other side of her mother's, she spent some time hanging up the clothes that would wrinkle, lining up the three pairs of boots she'd brought and laying out her makeup in an orderly arrangement. She didn't usually wear makeup, and today she could see why. Nobody appeared to have noticed that she looked any different at all.

Of course, she'd destroyed any favorable impression Jesse might possibly have by attacking his motives and those of his family. "Think before you speak," her mother used to say when Janie's big mouth got her in trouble at school. A lesson she clearly had yet to learn.

She touched up her mascara, shadow and powder anyway, then wandered across the room to stand at the window, gazing out over a psychedelic landscape of hotels, casinos, marriage chapels and traffic. She could just see the ridge of black mountains at the edge of the desert where a pink-and-gold sky anticipated the sunset. Her first night in Las Vegas, and she had no idea where to go or what to do.

Well, except find Jesse and apologize.

She knocked loudly on the door of the Cody suite, then waited, rubbing her thumbs over her fingertips in the nervous habit she'd never managed to conquer.

Jesse didn't answer the door. He might have gone out again. Maybe he'd planned dinner with friends, people who didn't accuse him of being the bad guy. He might have set up a date with a woman who knew how to keep her mouth shut.

Janie debated knocking again, but instead turned to go back to her room. She would check in on her mom, maybe get something to eat downstairs, then—

"Janie?"

She swung around with a gasp. Jesse stood in the open door, shirttail half in, half out, rubbing the top of his head.

"You were asleep." She stated the obvious. "I'm sorry. I didn't mean to wake you up."

"I didn't mean to fall asleep." He glanced at his watch. "Almost five o'clock. What's going on?"

She swallowed. "I, um, wanted to talk to you."

He tilted his head to the side and just looked at her for a few seconds. Then he took a deep breath and stepped back. "Come on in."

The huge suite she entered reminded Janie of the Cody homestead, with a living room featuring several different seating areas, a long dining table and chairs plus a big flat screen TV and music system.

"This is nice," she said, walking across the room to

look out the windows, which provided a view to the east. "I can see why your parents feel comfortable here."

"Yeah, we've been in this same room at the Finals as long as I can remember. What did you want to talk about?"

Facing him, she shoved her hands into her jeans pockets. "Well, obviously, I owe you an apology."

He shrugged one shoulder. "Not 'obviously.'"

Janie nodded. "Oh, yes. The kindest thing you could say was that I had to let off some steam, after the trip with Mom."

A half grin curved his lips. "I can say that."

"But whatever concerns I might have about your dad, I don't have any reason to make accusations that include you, Jesse. I'm sorry I blew up like that. You've been a real help today, and I'm grateful."

"Okay, then." He came close enough to put a hand on her shoulder. "Don't worry about it anymore. I know J.W. isn't an easy man to trust, especially for your family."

"But you are." She put her hand over his fingers as they rested against her body. "I've always trusted you."

Time stopped. Jesse's eyes widened as he looked down at her. A strange fluttering started up behind Janie's ribs as she focused on the weight and heat of his hand, the feel of his skin against her palm. Somebody took in a quick breath.

And then he backed away, letting his hand fall to his side. "So, what are your plans for your first night in Vegas? Gambling? Shopping? A show?"

Janie shrugged both shoulders, disappointed. "I don't have a clue. I'll take any recommendation you'd like to offer."

"What are Mark and Nicki doing?"

"Um, they might be staying in for the evening." She felt her cheeks heat up as she said it.

Jesse's flush showed that he took her meaning. "All these newlyweds are a pain in the butt for us single folks. Well, if you want to see a show, there's—"

She shook her head. "I'm not really big on going out by myself. I'll just get some dinner and sit with my mom."

He gazed at her for a few seconds. "Why don't the two of us go out together?"

AN HOUR LATER, JESSE EYED his reflection in the mirror, removed a hair from his black blazer and then met his own gaze.

"Dinner and a show," he told himself. "It's the least you can do for Elly's best friend. Not a big deal."

The trouble was, it felt like a big deal. He hadn't really meant to ask Janie out, in the social sense of the word, any more than he would ask his sister for a date. Hell, he'd seen Janie in her pajamas since she was a twelve-year-old sleeping over at the ranch. In all this time, he'd thought of her as a part of Elly's life. Not his.

Today seemed different…or maybe it had started last night, when she insisted on driving him home. He didn't recall ever being alone with Janie before, or really talking about anything more serious than a ball game on TV. Some of their conversations, last night and today, had been uncomfortable and explosive. But not dull. Janie didn't ignore issues, didn't gloss over the problems facing both of them. Jesse liked knowing where he stood and what he might be up against. He liked knowing what she thought and that she tried to fight fair.

The real shock was realizing that he'd never really

seen Janie before today. He'd always carried around this image of black pigtails, checked shirts and dirty hands. Elly, too—Jesse knew he tended to see her as the kid he remembered, with tangled hair and braces on her teeth, rather than the lovely adult woman she'd become.

Janie had changed, as well, and definitely for the better. Her sleek black hair, high cheekbones and bronzed skin revealed the Lakota blood she'd inherited from her mother. But her full, pouty mouth must have come from her dad's side of the family, along with her figure, rounded in all the right places. Despite her size—she couldn't be more than five-three—she struck Jesse as a curvy little package of dynamite.

In more ways than one. And that's what worried him.

He had enough complications in his life right now without adding any kind of relationship to the mix, let alone an attraction to his sister's best friend.

Or, for that matter, to his half brother's half sister.

So this would be just a friendly evening, he promised himself, walking down the hallway to Janie's door. Casual. Relaxed. No strings.

He knocked, Janie opened the door…and his gut lurched like a fish out of water.

I'm in serious trouble, here.

He could only hope his reaction didn't show on his face. "Ready to go?" As she stepped out and turned to make sure the door latched, he said, "You look nice tonight."

An understatement, if ever he'd made one. For the first time in both their lives, he was seeing Janie Hansen in a skirt—a swirly black skirt that revealed her sexy legs. She wore red boots with black stitching and black heels and a close-fitting red sweater with sequins across the shoulders. Her shiny black hair flowed like water down her back.

She looked, in a word, hot.

"Thanks," she said, smiling at him as she turned around. "I busted my budget on clothes for this trip. I almost never have a reason to dress up."

"That's too bad." The elevator doors opened as soon as he pushed the button, for which he was grateful. He could have kept shoveling on the compliments, which would only sabotage his "just friends" campaign. "What would you like for dinner?"

"I'm hungry enough to eat just about anything. You choose."

"How does Italian food sound?"

"Terrific."

A cab took them from their hotel to the Wynn Resort. Janie pressed her nose to the backseat window throughout the drive, exclaiming at the lights and sights of the Las Vegas street scene.

"You never imagine it quite this bright," she said as they walked through the Wynn Hotel entrance. "Or this tall. Or this crowded," she added, as a group of Asian tourists nearly ran over her.

Jesse put a hand at the small of her back as she edged toward him. "Sometimes people are watching what's around them instead of what's in front. Are you okay?"

"Sure. I can see why they're distracted. Just look at this place. Amazing."

A giant poster caught her eye and she stopped in her tracks. "Oh, wow. This is where he's performing?" One of the biggest stars in country music had come out of retirement to give concerts exclusively at the Wynn. "I've never seen him live. I love his music."

Jesse couldn't hide his grin. "Well, I guess that's good." Reaching into his breast pocket, he pulled out two tickets. "Because I just happen to have—"

"Jesse!" Janie screamed, and then threw her arms around his neck right there in the middle of the lobby. She had to jump to reach him, and he wrapped his arms around her, to keep them balanced.

The crowd flowed around them as they stood there for uncounted seconds, with Janie's breasts pressed tight against his chest and his head filled with the scent of spices that rose from her hair.

Finally, her arms loosened, and he had the presence of mind to ease his hold so she could slide back to the floor.

"I can't believe this." She had tears in her eyes. "How did you get tickets? I know his shows sell out months ahead of time."

With his hand back at her waist—and his blazer buttoned to hide the fly of his jeans—Jesse guided her on toward the restaurant. "Knowing we'd all be here, Dad bought a couple of tickets when they came up for sale. You never know who will want to do what, so he tries to provide lots of options."

Once seated at their table, Janie got up again almost immediately. "I want to check out the ladies' room. Be back in a few minutes."

The waiter stopped by while she was gone. Jesse ordered water and a whiskey for himself, then debated over what Janie's choice might be. He settled on a wine spritzer, which seemed to be what many of the women he dated would order in a place like this.

But when she returned, he saw her push the stemmed glass off to the side.

"You don't like spritzers?"

She shook her head. "I'm sorry, I don't drink alcohol. My dad was…you know, a problem drinker. I'm good with water."

"I'll get you something else." He raised his hand for the waiter. "What would you like?"

Most women would have protested and settled for what he'd ordered in an attempt to please him.

Janie tilted her head. "I'd love a ginger ale," she told him. "In a tall glass."

Jesse chuckled. "Coming right up, Ms. Hansen." He really appreciated a woman who knew exactly what she wanted.

Which made this particular woman all the more dangerous.

JANIE SAT MOTIONLESS long after the last note of the concert had faded, even after the rest of the audience, besides Jesse, had left the theater. She hated to move, or even breathe, if it meant breaking the spell of this most miraculous evening.

Then the lights went out.

Jesse grabbed her hand. "I think they're asking us to vamoose," he said, getting to his feet. "Let's hope we don't trip and fall on the way out."

The theater doors were still open, however, giving them plenty of light to negotiate from the first row, where they'd been seated, up the aisle and back into the main area of the resort.

In every direction, opportunities for gambling presented themselves—slot machines, card tables, roulette wheels, dice games.

"Want to take a chance?" Jesse stood at her elbow, watching as she looked around.

But Janie wasn't interested. "I don't have enough

faith in my own luck to risk my money like that. Besides…" she drew a deep breath, letting her eyes close for a second "…I just want to replay the music in my head."

The concert had been wonderful, a heartfelt performance by a megastar who also showed himself to be a warm and funny man.

But then, she'd been prepared to enjoy almost any kind of entertainment after sharing a dinner with Jesse Cody. She still couldn't quite believe the reality—she and Jesse, alone together, eating and talking about whatever came to mind. She'd filled him in on the restroom decor—fabulous—and he'd quizzed her about her pre-vet studies. Together they'd critiqued the movies scheduled to come out during the holiday season. Not once had they sat in silence, searching for something to say.

And she'd made him laugh—how about that for an achievement? She'd always thought Jesse never took enough time to laugh.

Now here they were, in a taxi again, and he was still holding her hand. His big fingers wrapped around hers, warm and secure like her favorite blanket back at home. If she moved her knee about two inches, she could touch his.

But Janie chose not to move. She'd already thrown herself at him once tonight, and she couldn't remember the moment without her face turning red. But she couldn't forget, either, the feel of his arms around her, the wall of his chest against her breasts, the aroma of his aftershave. Through all the excitement about the concert, she'd inhaled that scent as if her body needed it to survive.

When their cab pulled up at their hotel, Jesse's hand

slipped away from hers, reaching for his wallet. She waited and let him open her car door, then gave him her hand for help getting out. Hopefully, he'd keep it again on the elevator ride up.

Instead, he released her as soon as they entered the hotel lobby. Janie looked down at the floor to hide the disappointment in her face, so she didn't immediately notice the man plowing through the crowd in their direction.

Then her brother stopped directly in front of them. "Where the hell have you been?"

Even without holding his hand, she sensed Jesse stiffen beside her. She took a step ahead of him, getting between the two men. "We went to dinner and a show. I left a message for you."

"Fat lot of good that does, when you don't say where you're going. And I couldn't reach you on your cell phone."

"I didn't know." She took hold of Mark's wrist. "What's wrong? Is it Mom?"

He ran his free hand through his hair. "She's been hysterical for hours. When she woke up and you weren't available, she wouldn't eat, and the situation went downhill from there."

Janie headed toward the elevator at a fast walk. "Serena seemed to have everything under control…" She slammed the button with the heel of her hand. "She could have given Mom a sedative. I left the directions." Another punch at the up button produced no immediate result.

Mark pressed the button in his turn. "It's hard to give a sobbing, unrestrained woman a pill."

The doors slid open, finally, to reveal a compartment packed with people, adults overlapping at the shoulders and children fitted into the spaces below waist level. The process of emptying seemed endless.

A crowd of equal size followed Janie into the elevator. Pressed against the back wall between Jesse and Mark, she couldn't continue their discussion with so many listeners.

The last person didn't get off until the thirty-ninth floor.

When the panels parted on forty, Janie started running. The closed door to the suite brought her up short. She waited on tiptoe for Serena to answer her knock.

Just as she heard the lock release, big hands gripped her shoulders and forced her to turn around.

Behind her in the doorway, Serena said, "Miss Janie?" Inside the room, Abby moaned and sobbed.

Standing in front of her, Jesse shook his head. "You can't go in there, Janie. Not right now."

Mark came up beside them, pulled back his arm and knocked Jesse sideways with a punch to the shoulder.

"Mind your own business, Cody," he growled. "And get your hands off my sister."

Chapter Four

Jesse bounced off the wall and came back with his own punch ready.

Janie stepped in front of him. "Don't you dare."

He stopped, stared at her for a moment, then shook his head like a dog shaking off water. His hand fell to his side.

"You're right. Sorry." He flashed a furious glance over her shoulder to Mark. "I only meant that you should take the time to calm down and pull yourself together, before you went in to see your mom. But…" He looked around the circle of shocked faces—Nicki and Serena were watching, in addition to Janie and Mark. "But I didn't mean to intrude. I'll see you all tomorrow."

His boot heels thudded through the thick carpet as Jesse strode quickly down the hallway. The door to the Cody suite shut behind him with an impact just short of a slam.

Taking a deep breath, Janie turned and stepped past Serena into her mother's room. When Mark moved to follow, Janie stopped but didn't face him. "You've thrown your weight around enough for one night. Just stay with Nicki. I'll call you if we need you."

"What is your—"

He didn't get to finish because Serena closed the door in his face.

Janie looked at the older woman over her shoulder. "I knew I liked you." Then she peeled off her jacket, dropped it with her purse on the floor and went to sit beside her mother on the bed.

"I'm here, Mom," she crooned. "Shh, it's okay. Everything's fine."

Sure, Janie thought, remembering Jesse's face. Everything's just great.

JESSE HAD SET UP SOME practice time for Wednesday morning, on a ranch owned by a friend of his about a hundred miles out of Vegas into Utah. After spending half the night lying awake, thinking about Janie before and after her brother's intrusion, he sure as hell didn't want to think anymore.

So he set his music for a rowdy playlist—no love songs like the ones last night—and turned the volume high. All he wanted to do this morning was ride bulls and get as dirty as he possibly could.

The bulls were happy to oblige. He stuck five rides until the buzzer, but hit the sand early on three more.

"Those last three are my best." Chick Grady, the ranch owner, leaned on the arena fence as Jesse dusted himself off after that last fall. "Ain't nobody ever rode ol' Hoggy to the buzzer."

"Good to hear." Jesse climbed the fence and dropped down on the outside. "But I should have made it, if I plan to win."

"Stiff competition," Chick agreed. He stood five feet tall in his boots and displayed about a century's worth of wrinkles under the shade of his hat brim. "I have to say, yer not lookin' yer best this mornin'."

Removing the baseball cap he'd worn, Jesse bent over and dunked his head in a nearby horse trough to rinse the dirt off his face and cool down. Even in December, the sun shone strong in the Utah hill country. "Didn't get much sleep."

Chick snorted a laugh. "Gotta leave those ladies in Vegas to somebody else."

"I hear that." He caught the rag Chick threw him and wiped off his face and neck. "Easier said than done, sometimes."

"Decide what you really want." Chick spat a stream of tobacco into the dirt. "Then go get it."

"Right. Thanks, Chick. See you tomorrow."

Stripping off his filthy shirt, Jesse climbed into the truck in his T-shirt and aimed the windshield toward Las Vegas. He felt better for getting some fresh air and sunshine, for pitting his strength against an animal's and winning, more often than not. That was the fun part of bull riding, the part he enjoyed.

He whistled as he walked through the hotel's mid-afternoon horde and only grinned when the two women who joined him in the elevator stepped as far away from his dirt as they could manage. The hallway on the for-tieth floor was empty, and he sauntered to the suite in a better mood than he could remember for quite some time. Certainly since Mark Hansen had decided to com-plicate his life.

Then he unlocked the door and stepped inside to find a crowd of faces—worried, upset and downright angry—staring straight at him.

For some reason, the first person he focused on was Janie. She stood near the window, looking defiant and furious and apologetic, all at once.

"Well, it's about time." His dad's voice made itself

heard over several others. "Where the hell have you been?"

Like a balloon floating up against a prickly pear cactus, Jesse's mood deflated in that instant. He pulled off his baseball cap and rubbed a hand over his hair. "You know, I am really tired of hearing that question. Remember the good, old-fashioned word we use to greet somebody…what was it? Oh, yeah—hello."

"Hello, Jesse," his mother said. "We were surprised you weren't here when we arrived."

"I went over to Chick Grady's ranch. He let me ride a few of his bulls."

"How'd it go?" his dad barked.

Aware of Mark and Nicki sitting on the couch, Jesse shrugged. "Okay. I'll be going back tomorrow, get a little more loosened up." He surveyed the room, nodding to his brother Dex and his new wife, Josie, who were also part of the group. "Where's the rest of the family? I haven't seen Elly or Dusty or Walker since I got here. Not to mention the nephews." Dusty's son Matthew and Clay, Walker's wife's little boy, were two of his favorite people in the world.

"Dusty and Walker took the youngsters to the indoor pool," Josie told him. "Elly's working her horse and Maryanne went shopping at Cowboy Christmas."

His next questions would, no doubt, start up the fireworks. "Why didn't everybody go?" His gaze fell on Janie again as he asked the question, though she was the only one who didn't try to give an answer.

"Janie's talking about going home," he heard Mark say. "We've been trying to change her mind."

"That's her decision," J.W. declared. "She knows what's best." Trust his dad to take the easiest way out, for him, anyway. Having his ex-mistress down the hall would have to be awkward, even if his wife was being a saint about the whole situation.

"Don't you think Abby was better this morning?" Nicki appealed to Mark and then to Janie. "She seemed calmer at breakfast."

"Who knows what might happen in the next ten days?" J.W. pushed himself out of his chair and crossed the room to stand beside Jesse. "You don't have time to fly back, but we can hire a pilot."

No wonder Janie looked so stressed.

Jesse noticed that his mother hadn't contributed to the argument one way or the other. She sat without moving, staring down at her hands, folded in her lap.

As J.W. opened his mouth to make yet another ill-considered comment, Jesse held up a hand. Somewhat to his surprise, the room fell silent. Even J.W. paused.

"Seems to me," Jesse said carefully, "that Janie is capable of deciding what's best for her mother and herself without being harassed by folks with their own agendas." He glanced at Mark, to be sure he got that message, and saw the other man flush. "So why don't we all just let her have the time and space to consider her options? We can work out what needs to happen when she's made up her mind."

No one seemed to understand what he meant, because they just sat or stood where they were, staring at him. "That means you should all go back to your own rooms." He nodded at Nicki, and then at Josie and Dex. "Or go shopping. Whatever. Mom and Dad, you probably need to put your feet up for a while before dinner. After your long drive, that is."

His mother raised her head, met his gaze with her own cool blue stare and then nodded. "That's a good idea," she said quietly, getting to her feet. "We'll see you at six, Jesse." She withdrew to the master bedroom of the suite.

Jesse looked at his dad, raising his eyebrows in question. After a moment, J.W. followed his wife, muttering under his breath.

Dex and Josie left easily enough, and Nicki finally managed to get Mark to give up and go away. With the close of the door behind her brother, Janie's shoulders lifted on a deep breath.

"Thanks," she said, abandoning the window and coming into the center of the room. "I know they all meant well, but—"

"It felt like the inside of a pressure cooker when I walked in. I'm surprised you aren't as limp as a green bean."

"I might have been if you hadn't showed up." Her grin lacked its usual energy.

"Your mom had a really bad night?"

"Once I got back, she calmed down." Janie shrugged. "But what's the point of staying in Vegas if I have to be with her all the time? I might as well take her home and get back to work. I could use the paycheck." With her hair returned to its usual braid and her face pale from lack of sleep, as well as an absence of makeup, she seemed like a different person from the girl who'd hugged him in the Wynn lobby last night.

Jesse wondered how to reverse the change. "Maybe she just needs some time to adjust."

"Right—and maybe she'll get adjusted just in time for the whole thing to be over. Then we'll have a hard time getting her used to being at home again."

Suddenly, she covered her face with her hands. "Oh, that's a terrible thing to say. Don't listen to me, Jesse.

I'm really not bitter. I don't mind taking care of Mom, honest, I don't. It's just—"

Without thinking about it, he moved close enough to put his arms around her shoulders. "You carry a heavy load," he told her. "I know it's not easy, always being responsible for somebody else."

She leaned against him slightly. "I never expected to be my mom's caretaker. Her…her parent."

"I think most people in your situation would feel the same way. And handle it with less grace, less strength." Jesse realized now that he'd been listening over the past several years as his sister described Janie's struggle with her mother's deteriorating condition. He knew the things she'd had to cope with, though the two of them had never discussed the problem.

Only at this moment did he recognize how he admired her for the way she bore this burden without complaining or asking for help.

Janie took a deep breath and let it go, which seemed to ease her even closer against him. Jesse opened his hands against her shoulder blades, absorbing the size and shape of her body. She really wasn't very big, despite the curves. Her personality made her seem larger, somehow.

He lowered his chin, bringing his face close to the top of her head. The exotic scent of her hair made him smile and he pressed a kiss at the point where her bangs fell down across her forehead.

"Oh, I am sorry." A third voice broke the moment.

Instantly, Janie jumped away and whirled to stare at the intruder—his mother, standing at the doorway to her room.

Jesse clenched his teeth for a second. Could the day

get any worse? "Hey, Mom. Janie and I were…talking about her mother."

"I thought everyone had left," Anne Cody said, looking straight at him. Janie might as well not have been there.

"I do have to go," Janie said. "Thank you, Mrs. Cody. For…for everything." She brushed by Jesse and walked behind him to the door. In a low voice, she said, "I'll let you know what's going on." The lock clicked twice and she was gone.

His mother came into the living room and sat down in the same place she'd occupied before. Her stern expression warned Jesse what was coming. "Don't you think we have enough complications in our lives right now?" She pleated the sash of her robe between her fingers, but kept her eyes fixed on his face. "Don't I have enough to worry about?"

He sat down on the sofa across from hers. "What particular complication are you referring to?"

"What I just saw in this room."

Jesse rubbed his eyes with his fingertips. "I was offering Janie comfort, Mom. God knows she could use some, with all the trouble in her life."

"You kissed her."

He rolled his eyes. "Yeah, like I might kiss a little girl who dropped her ice cream cone." Not quite accurate, but he was too old to have to justify his kisses to his mother. "Maybe if somebody else gave her a little support, I wouldn't have to."

She understood his point. "I've conceded about as much as I can over this whole trip. Am I supposed to nurse the woman, too?" Unspoken but heard were the words *the woman who slept with my husband.*

"No." Jesse shook his head. "But you don't have to

give me grief for trying to improve the situation a little. You're the one who told me I had to fly them down here."

"Because your father committed us before I could say anything about it. I'm just trying to make sure our family stays together." She put a hand to her forehead, concealing her face. "All I've ever wanted to do is keep my family safe."

Once again, Jesse moved to put his arm around a woman in distress. "We're fine, Mom. You don't have to worry about any of us. We know where we belong."

His hug seemed to reassure her. She sat up and put a hand to his cheek. "I know you do, son. You're all great kids." She sighed, then got to her feet. "Maybe now I can rest. I just couldn't seem to settle until I'd talked to you."

He nodded. "I'll see you later, then."

She walked back to the bedroom door, and turned to give him a smile before going inside. Once the door shut, Jesse dropped his head back against the couch and closed his eyes. A sense of unease washed through him.

Something about his mother's anxiety hadn't quite rung true. Did she know about J.W.'s plans, about some kind of pressure he meant to put on Mark Hansen? Was she trying to warn him, or put up a smoke screen for his dad?

Either way, Janie seemed pretty determined to take her mother home, which would help foil anything J.W. might try.

Considering the possibility, Jesse had to admit that the extent of his disappointment seemed way out of proportion. He and Janie were barely even friends. And he had seldom participated in the social side of the National

Finals anyway. A night or two spent drinking with the guys, sure—once he was old enough to escape his dad's supervision. But events like the shopping extravaganza called Cowboy Christmas, the parties and receptions for visitors and Professional Rodeo Cowboys Association members, the tours and autograph booths and shows… none of those had been part of his NFR.

As far back as Jesse could remember, these ten days had been about the sport of bull riding. He'd spent his time observing the competitors as they practiced, talking to them to get tips on performance, then watching the events to see who won. When Cody bulls and horses were part of the draw, the week included taking care of the animals, too. Dinners with his dad's cronies and industry contacts usually occupied the evenings before each round of competition. His parents always threw a big party after the last show, which was their way of paying back a year's worth of favors to everyone they knew in the business.

This year, of course, he and Elly were actually competing for their event championships. They each had assigned times for autographing sessions, plus promotional appearances and press interviews, all of which only intensified the pressure and the responsibilities…. Bottom line—for the Codys, the National Finals Rodeo had never been about having fun. If Janie went home now, this year wouldn't be any different.

And that would be a good thing. Right?

WHEN JANIE RETURNED TO HER suite, she found Serena sitting alone in the living room.

"She's been sleeping since lunch. Would you like me to try to wake her now?"

"Let's see if she'll wake up on her own." They'd managed to get Abby through lunch without a dose of the sedative, and Janie would prefer to avoid more medication if at all possible. She felt bad enough at having dragged her mom across the country in this condition. The thought that Abby might spend the entire trip drugged into submission gave her daughter the shivers.

Going into her own room, Janie shut the door behind her and then leaned back against it, wondering what to do next. She'd heard the Codys discussing a dinner tonight with some of their business contacts. Mark and Nicki were going, along with most of the kids and their partners. She assumed Jesse, as head of the cattle operation, would be required to attend. Only Dusty, a screenwriter, was excused, since he had a meeting of his own with his agent and some film producers.

Maybe there was a good movie to watch on TV—just what she wanted to do on her first trip to Las Vegas.

At the thought, Janie squeezed her eyes shut to keep the tears from falling. She refused to resent her mother, absolutely would not give in to self-pity. Life offered opportunities and obstacles, and you just had to deal with whatever came your way.

"You could always study," she told herself aloud. "You do have that genetics final coming up in two weeks."

She'd been slowly working her way through courses at the community college, acquiring the credits she needed a few at a time until she could apply to the Colorado State University veterinary school. Their family budget had never allowed more than two classes a semester, and with her mom's declining health, she'd dropped back to taking one class at a time. At this rate, she'd be forty years old before she actually became a vet.

Or her mother could die soon….

"No!" Janie wasn't even going to think about the alternative. She stomped over to her bag, instead, pulled out her textbook and notebook and sat down in the armchair by the window. Where had she left off?

Oh, yeah. "Chapter Twenty-One—The Genetic Analysis of Populations and How They Evolve." So exciting.

A couple of hours passed as she became absorbed in the material. The sky outside her window had darkened considerably when Serena knocked on her door. "Janie? Your mother is awake."

Grateful to be released from her self-imposed study detail, Janie snapped her book closed and strolled into the living room, only to stop short when she saw her mom sitting on the sofa.

"Surprise!" Abby said. "It's me."

Janie grinned. "It sure is. You look great, Mom." Serena had evidently spent some time grooming her client—Abby's long hair was neatly braided, she looked like she'd had a bath or shower, and she wore yet another of the new lounge outfits Janie had purchased. Most important, she was actually, actively awake. And smiling.

Abby held out a hand to Janie and drew her to sit down on the cushion at her side. "What have you been doing all day?"

"I spent some time with the Codys this morning." Janie watched closely to see her mother's reaction. "I've been studying this afternoon."

Abby's eyebrows drew together. "The Codys. I know them, don't I?"

Maybe her failing memory would prove to be a blessing at this point. "They're friends of Mark's and Nicki's."

"Ah. Where is Mark? I'd like to have dinner with my two children." She squeezed Janie's hand.

"Um…Mark had a dinner to attend for the rodeo." Abby's face fell, and Janie tried to buffer the disappointment with an explanation. "You know how they do these publicity events for the competitors. Maybe tomorrow at lunch would work better." Unless they left town, of course.

Abby sighed, but didn't disintegrate into tears. "Well, I'm sure he's got a million things to do. When does he start riding bulls?"

"Tomorrow night is the first round."

"Oh, good. I can't wait to see him win."

Her delight was almost childlike, but Janie didn't doubt that Abby would love to see her son compete. She'd always supported his rodeo career, even when her husband—Janie's father but not, they now knew, Mark's—opposed the money and time Mark spent on the road.

Come to think of it, maybe Abby had approved of Mark's career exactly because of who his father really was. J. W. Cody had been a bull rider, before a serious injury introduced him to a pretty nurse named Anne— the future Mrs. Cody.

"But I'm here," Janie said, bringing her mind back to the present. "I'd love to have dinner with you. We can order room service and watch TV like we always do."

"Wonderful." Abby actually clapped her hands. "I want a steak."

Speaking to Serena a few minutes later, Janie shook her head. "She never cares what she eats. I can't believe she actually wants something specific."

"She may not eat anything when it gets here," Serena

warned her. "Just enjoy the good moments while they last."

That dinner turned out to be one of the best times Janie could remember with her mother in years. Abby did eat some of the steak, along with bites of potato and pieces of soft rolls. She commented on the images flitting across the television and laughed at commercials.

But she kept coming back to one subject. "I wish I could remember the Codys." She swirled a small piece of meat in a puddle of sauce. "Where have I met them?"

"Back home, Mom." Janie tried to avoid as many of the danger points as she could think of. "They have a ranch not far from Cody."

"It's a whole family? Mother, father and kids? How many?"

"You've met the oldest son, Jesse. He flew the plane that brought us here."

Again the puzzled look. "He's a pilot?"

"Um…yeah." Fortunately, another advertisement diverted Abby's mind from the subject. But the animated spirit she'd been displaying had started to fade, sending her back into the lethargy Janie knew too well.

"Tired, Mom?" She pushed the rolling table away from the couch. "Maybe you'd like to lie down for a while?"

Serena assisted Janie in lifting Abby to her feet and walking her into the bedroom. Like a toddler, Abby crawled across the bed, but Serena had turned the covers back, so she was able to lie down and be tucked in without a struggle. "I'll just sit with you awhile, Miss Abby," Serena volunteered. "That way if you need something, I'll be right here to help."

Janie saw that her mother was already almost asleep. Somehow the sight demoralized her even further. They'd had a fun dinner together…but after such a short time, they'd slid back into the same sad place.

With a deep breath, she left her mother's room and pushed the room service table into the hallway to be picked up. Returning to the room, she put out her hand to call housekeeping just as the phone rang.

She jumped and snatched up the receiver. "Hello?"

"Janie? This is Jesse."

Like she wouldn't recognize his voice after all these years? "Um…hi."

"You sound upset. Everything okay?"

"Sure. Of course. I just wasn't…wasn't expecting the phone to ring." Wasn't expecting a call from him. Ever.

"How's your mom tonight?"

She told him about dinner. "I can't believe how normal she seemed. Almost as if she'd never gotten sick."

"I'm glad you had such a good time with her. Maybe I should let you go—"

"No, it's okay." Janie tried not to sound too eager, or demanding. "Mom's gone back to bed. She started fading away again after we ate. She's probably asleep by now. It's after nine o'clock."

"I know." Background noises came through the phone—voices in conversation, along with the clink of glasses and some kind of piano music.

Janie recalled that he'd been scheduled for a business dinner. "Aren't you at a restaurant somewhere? With cattle buyers?"

"Yeah. But the dinner is breaking up. I left the table for a few minutes so I could check with you before it got too late."

"That's nice of you." She had to let him go—in more

ways than one. "We're doing okay here, so you should get back to your guests."

"Wait a second." He didn't say anything for much longer than that. And then he asked, "Uh…what are you doing for the rest of the night?"

Janie blinked, shook her head violently, stared hard at the phone receiver and then put it back to her ear. "I'm sorry. What did you say?"

The words came to her slowly, distinctly. "Do you have plans for tonight?"

"Tonight is almost over, Jesse."

"Depends on your definition. There are places in this town, like Fremont Street, where tonight doesn't end until the sun rises on tomorrow."

"That's a pretty wild point of view." And her heart pounded at the thought of what he might really be asking.

"I told you this was a crazy place, during one of the craziest weeks of the year. Do you want to see what I mean?"

"You're planning to go out? Now?"

"If you'll come with me."

Chapter Five

Fremont Street, the echo of Las Vegas's rowdy past, lived up to its reputation. And then some.

But as far as Jesse was concerned, the most spectacular sight of the evening had to be the woman walking beside him, holding his hand.

Her dark eyes wide with excitement, her lips parted in surprise, laughter or amazement, Janie moved easily through the crowd, finding something new to investigate every yard or two. She got more than her share of glances from the guys they encountered, and Jesse wasn't sure whether to be proud or just punch them out.

But he couldn't blame them. Under a white Stetson hat, her shiny hair swung like silk down past her shoulder blades. Lacy silver earrings with turquoise stones dangled from her earlobes, tinkling with every move of her head. She wore a white jacket, fringed along the sleeves and across the back yoke, with a low-necked turquoise top underneath. Jesse's favorite part of the outfit was the slim black skirt and shiny black boots with white stitching. All these years, Ms. Janie Hansen had been hiding a terrific pair of legs under her everyday jeans.

"There it is!" She halted, looking up. "The light show is starting again."

Jesse followed her gaze for a few minutes, watching computerized images composed by millions of tiny lights dance over a canopy stretching the length of five football fields. Then he let his eyes return to Janie herself, taking pleasure in the delight on her face at the holiday-themed program and synchronized music. She had a great smile—why had he never realized that before now?

Maybe because she rarely smiled when she was at home? Not around him, anyway.

She'd refused his invitation when he called, explaining that she needed to stay at the hotel in case her mother woke up. Then, ten minutes later, she'd called him to say she'd changed her mind. Jesse had decided not to ask why—he knew better than to give her a chance to review the decision. He'd allowed her ten more minutes to get ready before knocking on her door. Serena had his cell phone number, and would call immediately about the slightest problem.

Midnight had come and gone, and they'd been on Fremont Street for a couple of hours, now. Janie made him check his phone every five minutes, but so far there had been no calls.

Instead, they'd gambled a little, stepped into a few clubs for drinks and dancing and visited the traditional Las Vegas Christmas tree. Janie studied each of the huge neon signs rescued from Las Vegas landmarks and stopped to read every information poster along the way. Jesse was glad he'd worn his most comfortable boots.

The show above them came to its cheerful conclusion, accompanied by applause from the wall-to-wall crowd along the street. Still grinning, Janie came back to earth.

"I'm thirsty." She shouted to be heard over the noise. "And I'd like to sit down for a while."

Jesse nodded. "Sounds good." Taking the lead, he pulled her after him as he wove through the press of people toward a sign promising Cold Beer and Hot Jazz. Since the other nearby option offered Beautiful Babes, he figured this was the safer choice.

The noise level dropped as soon as they crossed the threshold, which was a definite improvement.

"Whew." Janie rubbed her hands over her ears. "Will I ever hear a pin drop again?"

The hostess, dressed in skintight black leather, showed them to a round table with booth seating, in a room so dark he couldn't see the other walls. Jesse chuckled as he slid in after Janie. "These places are a little claustrophobic, don't you think? I'm getting homesick for an empty prairie and the whistle of wind coming off the mountains."

"But this is much more exciting." She glanced at the empty stage. "A real Vegas dive. I hope the band is coming back."

They asked the waitress when she arrived. "Sure," the blonde said, not looking at them. Her pink tank top and white satin boxer shorts barely corralled all of her physical assets. "What'll you have?"

Jesse ordered beer and Janie asked for her favorite ginger ale. As the waitress left, Janie nearly choked as she started laughing. "She must have spent a fortune on plastic surgery. Wow."

"I notice a lot of…uh…enhancements walking around Vegas," Jesse said, trying to keep a straight face.

"I bet you do." She stuck her tongue out at him. "Do

you suppose they have food? I just realized I'm hungry, too."

When the drinks arrived, they ordered a plate of tiny cheeseburgers and a side of fries. The band members—all women, all dressed like the waitress and with similar "enhancements," as Janie pointed out in a giggling whisper, wandered onto the stage one at a time, made a few startling noises with their instruments and then started to play.

Jesse widened his eyes at the sound, and a glance at Janie showed her equally impressed. The hot, smoky voice of a sax threaded through the shadowed room, joined by a growling trumpet and throbbing bass. The waitress dropped off a plate of perfect burgers and crisp fries, proving the food as good as the music.

Gradually, couples materialized on the dance floor, swaying to the music. Jesse watched and listened, knowing he should keep his butt solidly in the seat underneath him. Dancing with Janie, in this situation, would be a very bad idea.

Sure, they'd danced earlier. Jumping around to rock tunes or boot scootin' with a country crowd posed no real threat. But this sex-driven music required a totally different style. This kind of dancing would generate all the wrong signals.

Not for everybody, maybe. But between him and Janie…oh, yeah.

So he stuck to the booth and kept his hands wrapped around the cold beer on the table. Beside him, Janie sat with her chin propped in her hands, eyes half-closed and body swaying with a sultry rhythm. Jesse took a deep breath and ordered another beer when the blonde waitress drifted by.

In the end, her lips did Jesse in—Janie's lips, plump

and rosy, slightly parted as she drifted with the music. His body ached to move. He needed a woman in his arms. This woman. To hell with the consequences.

He swiped his palms over his jeans, then touched her hand.

Her lids lifted, slowly, and she looked at him.

"Want to dance?"

Jesse saw his own thoughts go through her mind, read surprise and desire fighting against caution. Maybe he could count on Janie's willpower, since his own had failed.

But then her smile widened, and he knew desire had won. She nodded, without saying a word.

They came together on the dance floor. Her high boot heels brought her head to the level of his shoulder, aligning their bodies just right. She put an arm around his waist and her left palm against his, while he slid his hand from her shoulder to the perfect hollow in the curve of her back. Lucky for him, the room was warm and she'd left the fringed leather jacket at the table. The fabric of her shirt only lightly veiled her warm skin.

Bodies swayed around them. Jesse shifted side to side, slid a foot forward or back, without traveling anywhere at all. The temperature climbed—or maybe it was just his temperature. Having Janie this close, feeling her breasts curving into his ribs, her knees pressing and releasing against his, tested the limits of his control. Nothing would happen—he knew that. They were out in public, for God's sake.

Then Janie lifted her head to stare into his face. The arch of her throat, flowing into the low V of her shirt and the shadow at its point…the silver earrings dangling from tiny earlobes…silky hair falling back from her face, revealing the shape of her bones and the smooth skin beneath her ears…

Those red, red lips.

Jesse didn't think about it. He just bent down and claimed the kiss he craved.

JANIE KNEW SHE WASN'T asleep. So how could she be having The Dream?

Since she was fourteen, every so often she would wake in the middle of the night with a sweet flush throughout her body and a warm tingle in her lips that revealed where her mind had been. The setting was always different—the clothes, occasion, atmosphere and music changed every time. If she lay quiet, though, the images would come back—herself somewhere, in Jesse's arms. The kisses they shared seemed as real as the pillowcase under her cheek or the wind whispering through her window.

Tonight felt exactly the same, as his mouth pressed into hers and his lips moved against her sensitive skin until her knees almost gave way.

He would catch her, in that case, with his arms supporting her body, pulling her tighter against him as they shuffled on the dance floor. The sax wrapped its sinuous tune around them, murmuring suggestions that embraced every wish she'd ever made concerning Jesse Cody.

If they didn't stop soon, those wishes would all come true. In public.

Jesse's hands were moving over her back, down to her waist and below. She gasped as his fingers stroked over the backs of her bare legs, just below the hem of her skirt. His hand came to her head, then, and held her still while he kissed her until she couldn't even breathe, let alone think.

After some unknown length of time, the music ended, with a long whinny on the trumpet that sent a shiver up Janie's spine.

"Gonna take another break," the bass player said into her mike. "Back soon."

Aware that people were walking past them, Janie managed to step back, away from Jesse's body. She had to think hard about which direction to take to reach their table, and what to do when she got there.

While she was still puzzling, Jesse came up beside her.

"Restroom," she croaked. "Then we'd better go."

"Right." His voice didn't sound any steadier than hers.

She grabbed her jacket from the booth and walked a crooked path toward the hostess station to ask directions, then made a U-turn toward the back of the club to find the ladies' room. Inside, gray fluorescent light showed her a marginal standard of cleanliness and herself in the mirror looking heavily drugged. Smudged mascara ringed her eyes. Her cheeks were pale but her lips were bright red.

Been kissed lately? she asked herself.

She did what she could to repair the damage and wiped a wet paper towel over her throat and the nape of her neck, trying to cool down. Too bad the fire was all internal and impossible to quench.

Back in the club, Jesse stood by their table. "Ready?" he asked, without the smile in his eyes she'd been enjoying all night long.

Janie nodded and blazed a trail toward the exit. What would happen now, she couldn't predict. Stepping into the cool night air tumbled her from a daze of passion into a state of nervous energy, as if she'd had too much coffee. The noises seemed louder, the colors brighter. She wanted to do something crazy.

Like make love with Jesse all night long.

Out on Fremont Street, the family crowd had thinned considerably, leaving the casinos as the center of attention. Plenty of "enhanced" girls still walked the streets. After they sidestepped a woman bargaining with her current customer, Janie blew out a breath. "I guess for some people this is just the middle of the workday."

Jesse had his hand pressed securely against her back. "You have to be truly dedicated to continue gambling after 2:00 a.m."

"I can understand some kinds of addictions." As they passed a casino, the man at an outdoor slot machine begged the woman next to him for another coin. "But gambling?"

Beside her, Jesse shrugged. "The search for your next adrenaline rush, I guess. Risking all you've got on the next round. Sorta like riding bulls."

She gave him a sideways glance. "Sounds like you're reconsidering your choice of a hobby."

When he didn't say anything, she gave him a longer look. His eyes had narrowed and his mouth was hard. They walked past several shops before he answered. "Not until next Friday night, anyway. Once I win, then maybe I'll quit."

She waited to speak again until they'd passed underneath the neon sign for Fremont Street. Immediately, the noise level diminished. "What if you don't win?"

"Not an option." He stared straight ahead without meeting her gaze. Instead of holding her hand, he'd put a good yard of empty space between them.

His standoffish attitude provoked her to attack. "Mark's good."

He clenched his fists at his sides. "I'm better."

"Are you luckier?"

Finally, he turned to face her. "Are you trying to start an argument because I kissed you?"

"No, of course not." Then she thought about it. "Maybe."

He rolled his eyes and put up a hand to attract a nearby cab. "If you think you have to make me angry to keep me from hitting on you again, don't worry. I won't."

The cab pulled up and Jesse opened the door for her to get in. With her head reeling as if she'd just been slapped, Janie walked around to the street side of the car and opened her own door. They both got in and slammed their doors at the same time.

Jesse turned sideways to face her. "Look, I didn't mean—"

Janie held up a hand. "I don't want to discuss it with an audience."

He glanced at the driver and dropped back into the seat. "We will discuss it," he muttered.

"That's what you think," she said, gritting her teeth.

At their hotel, Jesse didn't wait for her to slide out on his side, but the cab driver jumped out and opened her door. That gave Janie a chance to score—she handed him a couple of bills and told him to keep the change.

Jesse took her arm as they walked into the lobby. His grip wasn't gentle. "You paid him four times too much."

She jerked out of his grasp and hit the elevator button. "So he can go home early tonight."

Unluckily, they had the elevator all to themselves. "I didn't mean to insult you." Jesse turned to face her, leaning sideways against the back wall. "Back at the club—that was a serious mistake. My fault, I admit it. But you know I'm right."

The fortieth floor seemed very far away, and the elevator had slowed to a crawl. Janie refused to look at him. "Do I?"

"Yes. We've already got one family mess on our hands. Do we need another?"

"This would be a mess? You and...me?" Starting to cry while he was talking to her—that would definitely be a mess.

Jesse sighed. "Your brother is my brother. My dad and your mother...it's all wrong."

"If you say so." She stepped to the front of the car, showing him her back, hiding her face. He only spoke the truth. It was her problem if she didn't want to hear it.

"I've got all the complications I can handle right now, Janie. Maybe once the Finals are over—"

The doors slid open and she left as quickly as she could, all but running down the hall. "Great. Give me a call when your schedule lets up."

His footsteps pounded after her. "Janie, stop."

"No, really." She'd been digging out her room key since they'd left the lobby. Now she fitted it into the door. "I had a great evening. Let me know when you can work me in. I'll always jump at the chance to enjoy a charity date with the high-and-mighty Jesse Cody."

"Tonight wasn't about charity."

"Could've fooled me." She pushed the door open, then turned back and gave a snap of her fingers. "Oh, wait—you did fool me. Good job. And good night."

Janie shut the door in his face, then shut herself into her room, vowing to ignore that same high-and-mighty Jesse Cody for the rest of the trip. If she spent all her time in the hotel, that might be possible.

No matter where she was, though, she wasn't sure she would manage to ignore her aching heart.

THE CODY BROTHERS STAYED out late after the third go-round on Saturday night, sending the women and children and even their father back to the hotel while they went for steaks, beer and pool.

"I invited Mark," Dex told them once they'd ordered. "He said he needed to get back and check on his mom."

Jesse gritted his teeth and swallowed a protest.

But his reaction hadn't gone unnoticed. Dex frowned at him. "He's part of the family, whether we like it or not."

Walker set down his beer mug. "He's not a bad guy. A little on the prickly side."

"I'd be prickly," Dusty said, "in his place."

"I guess you're not talking about the fact that I won tonight," Jesse growled.

Dusty grinned at him. "I guess not. He's no happier about this situation than you are, big brother."

"Why should he be unhappy? He just came into part of a fortune."

Will Jackson, Elly's fiancé, leaned forward. "How about suddenly having four brothers who wish they'd never heard your name?"

Walker held up a hand. "I'm not part of this fight. I've got all I need with Paula and Clay."

"Don't look at me, either." Dusty cut into his steak and savored a bite before continuing. "My screenplays are getting attention in Hollywood. I don't have time for a family feud."

"Jesse's the one who's mad." Dex eyed him sternly. "The rest of us have always had to share. Maybe it's time you learned, too."

Dusty whistled. "That's a low hit, man. Jesse's one of the good guys."

Now the twins were glaring at each other. "Not when he acts like a dog in the manger," Dex said.

Jesse had lost his appetite. He pushed his chair back from the table. "I'm going to shoot some pool." Stalking from the dining room, he made sure to bring his beer mug with him and planned to have it refilled often.

His brothers gradually joined him, Walker first. "Calmed down yet?"

"Don't know what you're talking about." Jesse fired a ball into the side pocket.

"I suspect you're still struggling with the idea that Dad's human. Like all of us."

"I'm still struggling with the fact that he cheated on his wife, who just happens to be a hell of a woman." His next shot sent the ball over the bumper to bounce on the floor and roll underneath a chair by the wall. "Don't you care how much Mom must have been hurt?"

Walker stepped up to the table and bent over to set up his shot. "She forgave him, Jesse. She's been married to him for more than thirty years. If she could manage, why can't you?"

"She thought they'd left it behind them. Instead, it... he is sitting right in front of them. That's got to be painful."

Dex swung in on his crutches, souvenirs from a bad fall and recent knee surgery. "You're assuming they didn't know Mark was Dad's son before all this came up."

Mouth hanging open, Jesse stared at his brother. Even Walker looked surprised. "You think they knew? When we were kids?"

"Think about it," Dusty said, straddling a chair. "Three of us like Mom—shades of blond with blue eyes, or green."

"Elly's eyes are greenish blue," Will put in. "Kinda like the ocean."

Along with his brothers, Jesse rolled his eyes at the dreamy expression on Elly's fiancé's face.

"Whatever," Dusty said. "But Mark Hansen looks like Dad—whip thin, dark hair and that lean face."

"So?"

Dex heaved a sigh. "Come on, Jesse. Markton's a small town. If you'd been with a woman who had a baby—say, about nine months later—wouldn't you wonder a little? Suppose her husband was blond, which Mr. Hansen was, and the kid grew up dark-haired. Wouldn't you think twice?"

"Abby Hansen is—"

"Is dark." Dusty nodded. "But Mark's face is the image of Dad's. I can't believe neither he nor Mom noticed. I think they knew from early on, if not the beginning."

"And ignored him? You think they could do that?"

Walker said, quietly, "Why else would Dad be trying so hard to make amends?"

After that question, the rowdy fun the brothers had been planning to have together never materialized. Jesse couldn't get over the possibility that his parents had deliberately ignored a Cody child. Not long after midnight, with his third straight loss at the table, he told his brothers good-night. Taking one more chug from his beer mug, he set out to walk the long blocks back to the hotel.

As he walked, he could only conclude that he'd made the right choice as far as Janie was concerned. Until he could get the family's situation straightened out, he didn't have room in his life for romance. Certainly not a lasting relationship.

And with Janie, he realized suddenly, he wouldn't want any other kind.

GOING BACK TO HIS ROOM after an autographing session a week later, Jesse heard the call come from down the hallway.

"Hey, cowboy! Wait up." Not Janie's voice.

He turned on his heel in the hall to see Nicki coming his way. "Hello there, Mrs. Hansen. You're looking pretty happy these days."

"I am happy, thank you." She walked with him to the suite and stepped inside while he held the door. "Mark and I are just...well, terrific together."

"Glad to hear it. Can I get you something to drink?"

"No, thanks." She settled herself on a sofa. "I guess you're feeling pretty good, too, sitting in the number two spot after six go-rounds."

"Sure." He pulled a beer out of the refrigerator and twisted off the cap. "I'd be happier as number one, but your husband's got a lock on that until tonight, at least."

Nicki smiled. "Yeah, he has been riding really well. I'm proud of both of you." The smile faded. "But I'm worried about you, too, Jesse. What's going on?"

Great. Just frigging great. He'd already been "talked

to" by his mother, his three brothers and his baby sister. Now his former best friend had decided to take a shot. "What do you mean?"

She held up a finger. "You're too quiet. You're drinking more than I've ever seen you drink." Finger two. "You smile about once a day, when you're talking with the little boys. Or signing autographs."

"That would be at least a hundred times a day. My hand is about to fall off."

She frowned at his interruption. "You're not eating much." Finger three. "You're losing weight." Four.

"I'm fine."

"And you brush off anybody in the family who tries to find out what happened between you and Janie."

"That's because nothing happened between me and Janie."

"I'd believe that except for the fact that she's as miserable as you are."

"How can you tell, since she never leaves the hotel room?"

Nicki stared at him with narrowed eyes. "Why are you avoiding each other?"

"Ask her. I'm just doing what I came here for—riding bulls."

"Did you do something to hurt her, Jesse?" On her feet now, Nicki came to stand in front of him with her hands fisted on her hips. "Mark's tried to talk to Janie, but she hasn't said a word."

"That's the definition of *nothing,* sweetheart." When he tried to turn away from her, Nicki caught his arm.

"Don't you try to B.S. me, Jesse Cody. We've been best friends too long for this kind of game."

"Yeah, but you're a married woman now, Nicki. Married, in fact, to the man I've been competing against as far back as I can remember, the man who turns out to be the proof that my dad is a cheat. You'll have to forgive me if I'm not as comfortable with you as I used to be. A hell of a lot has changed recently."

Her green eyes widened. "You're saying we're not friends anymore?"

"I'm saying that your husband would not be very happy to know we're alone together right now. And do you really expect me to spill my guts on any given topic when what I say could get back to Mark? You know better, Nicki, however much you might be hoping for something different."

Tears spilled onto her cheeks. Her mouth opened, but no sound came out.

Jesse put his arm around her shoulders. "It's okay, Nicki. You love him, and you had to make a choice. I'm not blaming you. And we're still friends. Just not best friends. That's between you and Mark now."

Wiping her cheeks with her fingertips, she sniffed, then nodded. "We are best friends. I just…Jesse, I've never seen you so down for so long."

Keeping hold of her, he walked her toward the door. "You do not have to worry about me. I'm okay, and I'll be even better when the balance tips in my favor and I get that big gold buckle to wear home on my belt." He opened the door. "So if you're going to tell that husband of yours anything, just tell him to prepare to lose. 'Cause it's going to happen."

She was smiling when he shut the door, which was what he'd hoped to accomplish. He leaned back against the panel and emptied the remainder of the bottle with a couple of gulps, then headed to the fridge for another.

Nicki had the facts right, of course. He wasn't hungry, couldn't sleep and started every day with the first of many brown bottles in his hand. Since Janie wouldn't answer his phone calls and refused to see him in or out of her hotel room, what else could anyone expect?

At least he was staying on the bulls. His scores weren't quite as high as Mark's, but he still had four nights to make up the difference. The number three guy, his friend Sandy Thorpe, was breathing down his neck, but with all the money Jesse had made during the year, he could win as long as he put in four solid rides.

The thought took him back to last Wednesday night outside Fremont Street with Janie. She'd generated an argument about whether or not he should quit riding bulls…why? Because he'd kissed her? But when he promised to leave her alone, she only got more upset. What the hell did the woman want?

He knew what he wanted…more of the same. More of Janie's mouth under his, more of her body pressed against him—more of all of her, somewhere private and quiet. Surely she could tell how she'd made him feel.

And surely she knew how big a problem that kind of relationship between them would create. He hadn't even figured out how to deal with having Mark Hansen in his life, in his family. How could he get involved with a woman when he wasn't sure he knew himself anymore?

He'd hated Mark Hansen since they were kids. Now, with no more than a blood test to signify the difference, they were brothers. But Jesse had standards for the way he treated his brothers and the way he felt about them. Nothing to do with Mark Hansen fit those standards.

Nicki might have switched loyalties. She was free to do that, and Jesse truly wished her well.

But Janie wasn't free to change her affections. Mark was her brother, her protector, the boy she grew up with and the man who helped her deal with her mother. Until Jesse and Mark could resolve their differences, asking Janie to choose between them was simply not fair. Not right.

And…since every cell in Jesse's body rebelled at the thought of taking second place to his father's illegitimate son…

Not possible.

ANNE CODY WATCHED JESSE as the family gathered in their hotel suite after the seventh Finals performance. His mellow voice and deep laughter sounded several times as he traded jokes with his brothers. He'd won tonight's go-round, which put both Jesse and his father in a terrific mood.

He was her favorite son, which she could admit only to herself. All her children were precious, of course, and she wouldn't trade her daughter, Elly, for anything in the world. Each boy was endearing in his own way, and she loved them fiercely.

But Jesse…he'd been a precious gift, a blessing she'd once doubted she'd would ever experience. A miscarriage at six months of pregnancy with her first baby had left her deeply depressed, wondering if she would ever bear a child. John Walker's infidelity, on top of the tragedy, had brought her close to suicide.

His abject apology, his promise to be faithful and his unconditional love had drawn her back from the precipice. They had looked forward from that point on. A year later, she'd given birth to a perfect baby boy— Jesse. John Walker had been ecstatic to have a son who would inherit his name and the Cody tradition.

Now, there was Mark, an older son with a different last name. John Walker was determined to bring him into the family, but refused to consider the damage he might cause.

A financial settlement would be so much easier.

Instead, her firstborn had to stand by while his best friend married his closest rodeo rival and the man who supplanted him as the oldest Cody son. No wonder Jesse was tense these days. He must be thinking he couldn't win on any front.

"Annie? Are you okay?" John Walker snapped his fingers in front of her face. "Wake up, girl."

She called up a smile as he dropped down beside her on the couch. "Sorry. Just thinking about the old days."

"A waste of time. We should be looking forward. We're in for a bull riding win this year, one way or the other. Jesse and Mark are running neck and neck at this point." His dark eyes searched her face. "Do you like him?"

She knew he meant Mark. "I'd say he's a nice young man."

The severe line of his mouth expressed disappointment. "That's a prissy answer, Annie. You know I care what you think about him."

"I've only had about a week to talk with him, John Walker. I can't know him very well when rodeo is the only topic of conversation."

John Walker stared at her for a moment. "You're willing to keep trying, aren't you?"

Anne shrugged. "I don't see what else we can do at this point." She pressed her lips together, holding in an anger she thought had been doused thirty years ago.

"I made two huge mistakes, Annie. First, I strayed from my marriage. Then I ignored my son, pretending that Abigail's baby wasn't mine when my gut told me different.

"Now I'm trying to set things right." He covered the back of her hand with his palm. "I'm glad I get that chance."

She forced herself to relent, to accept his need for restitution. "I understand, John Walker." Leaning close, she pressed her cheek to his shoulder. "If you'll give it some time, I think we'll all be able to accept Mark as part of the family."

His arm came around her shoulders, and he kissed the top of her head. "I love you so much," he whispered. "Make your excuses in a little while and come to bed."

He squeezed her hand, said good-night to the kids and went into their bedroom. Anne stayed, still thinking, until her children and their partners headed to their own rooms.

Having admitted his mistake, John Walker had set about making amends. He might be thirty years late with the effort, but he wanted Mark to be a Cody in every sense of the word. With his world set to rights, he felt he could face the future without flinching.

Watching the effect on her children, however, Anne was not convinced. Though Jesse's dilemma was the worst, discovering their father's infidelity had shaken all of them. This disillusionment was what she'd tried to prevent when she'd given him the ultimatum. He could have a family with her, she'd told him thirty years ago, or with Abigail. Not both. As she'd hoped, John Walker had chosen her and they'd made a beautiful life together.

But Anne was beginning to fear that her efforts to protect her family might, in the end, destroy it instead.

Chapter Six

Day ten. One last ride for the world championship.

Janie settled her mother into a chair in the luxury box the Codys always purchased for the National Finals. In what seemed to be a miracle, Abby had been more like herself during the past week than Janie could remember for several years. They'd even managed to take a couple of excursions together—shopping with Elly at the Cowboy Christmas Sale and a ride out into the desert with Mark and Nicki. Plus their nightly visits to the Thomas & Mack Center to watch Mark and Elly compete.

And Jesse, of course.

Now the final round of rides was just minutes away. Abby had taken an afternoon nap and was feeling good. She gazed around the stadium, apparently enjoying the mass of people and the noise.

"Does Mark ride next?" She caught Janie's hand. "Is it Mark's turn?"

"Not yet. First the barrel racing—we get to see Elly."

"Oh, good." As Abby surveyed their surroundings, Anne and J. W. Cody entered the box and took their seats across the aisle, next to Nicki's dad. She turned to Janie with a puzzled expression. "Who's that sitting with us?"

"Elly's mom and dad. The Codys. We saw them earlier, remember?"

Her mom gave a vague smile. "Oh…yes. Of course." Then she resumed her survey of the crowd.

Anne Cody had been a gracious hostess this week— she'd stopped by every day to ask after Abby and make sure they had everything they needed. That can't have been easy, given the trouble between them. But then, Janie had always known where Jesse got his strong sense of honor.

The seat beside her creaked and she turned to see her sister-in-law sitting down. "Hey, Nicki. How's Mark feeling?"

"Good." Nicki nodded hard, as if to convince herself. "I think. I mean, they all put on a show for each other, pretending they're too tough to be worried about a little thing like the National Finals. But Mark really does feel good, and he's confident that he can ride the bull he's drawn. Xerxes is his name."

"I've heard of him." Statistics were kept on the top bulls just as on the top riders, and the animals often had their own fans. "He's tough, but tends to play fair. That's a great draw."

She couldn't ask about Jesse because she didn't deserve to know. Sticking to her vow, she'd avoided him since last Wednesday night by staying with her mother in their suite and bypassing any Cody gathering where he might show up. That had been, of course, most of the Cody gatherings.

But since she wasn't a family member, that didn't matter to them anyway.

She'd gotten out of the hotel occasionally by herself

when her mother slept or when Mark and Nicki were with her. She'd taken Mark's truck one afternoon and driven aimlessly around Las Vegas, trying to get a feel for the city that didn't include casinos and money. She hadn't discovered much else, and instead had found herself getting progressively more homesick.

Tomorrow, thankfully, she would be going home. Janie had stretched the credit card balance a little further and bought plane tickets for herself and her mother. She couldn't fly with Jesse again. Not the way things stood between them.

So, regardless of who won and who lost tonight, she could say goodbye to Las Vegas in the morning and get back to her regular life—her regular life without any possibility of a relationship with Jesse Cody. Things simply didn't work between them. She knew that, now.

"Janie?"

She jumped, having been lost in her own thoughts and oblivious to whatever Nicki was saying. "I'm sorry. What did you say?"

"I said, I'm not feeling so optimistic about Jesse's chances tonight. Mark has my support, of course, but I'd like to see Jesse do well. Instead he looks terrible." Nicki stared at her a moment. "So do you."

"Thanks so much." Janie frowned, her arms crossed over her chest. She did not want to have this conversation.

But Nicki did. "What happened between you two? You seemed to be getting along and then…boom…you weren't anymore."

"That about sums it up."

"What did he do to make you mad?"

Kissed me and then backed away as if he'd tasted poison, for one thing.

She took a deep breath and prepared to lie. "Really, there's nothing to tell, Nicki. We just realized we don't get along. Some people are meant to be together, like you and Mark. Some of us, like me and Jesse, aren't. End of story."

"I can tell a lie when I hear it, Janie. But if that's all you'll say, so be it." With a sniff, Nicki stood up and moved over to sit with her dad. Janie was sorry to make Nicki angry, but she was still trying to explain to herself what had happened with Jesse. She couldn't possibly make it clear to someone else.

By showtime, the entire Cody family had arrived in the box—those not performing, at least. Janie hadn't seen them all in one place for years, and the collection made quite an impression. Walker, the next oldest after Jesse, had brought his new wife, Paula, and her little boy, Clay. Dex arrived, with his fiancée, Josie, and their son, Matt—the first Cody grandchild, whose father happened to be Dex's twin, Dusty. Janie had felt pretty dressed up in a short skirt and red silk shirt, with her dressiest black-and-red Lucchese boots, but Dusty's fiancée, from Los Angeles, Maryanne, had joined him tonight. Now *there* was real style.

Finally, William, Elly's fiancé, arrived. After shaking hands with all the men and greeting the ladies, he came to sit beside Janie.

"Elly wanted me to sit with you," he said, squeezing her hand. "She'll be up here after she rides and she says she has something to give you."

"Do you know what?"

"No clue." He turned toward the arena. "Here come the flags."

The opening ceremony featured riders carrying flags from every state represented by the competitors, plus the national flag, performing a series of complicated maneuvers on horseback. Once they lined up across the arena, a major country music star appeared onstage to sing the national anthem. Through her tears, Janie saw most of the folks around her wiping their eyes.

Then, at last, the final go-round could begin.

After ten quick runs around the barrels, the crowd in the Cody box was happy, though not jubilant. Elly had placed second for the national title.

"I want you to know," Janie told Elly when she finally arrived during the saddle bronc event, "that I've beaten that girl several times in the last couple of years. And you can beat me two times out of three, so this was just a lucky break for her. You're still the best."

Elly gave her a huge hug. "Thanks, friend. I love you." Pulling back, she winked at William. "And I have a present for you, Ms. Janie." Reaching into the neckline of her shirt, Elly started pulling on a cord that proved to be attached to her identification badge and competitor's admission card.

She closed Janie's hand around the badge. "Stuff that black braid of yours up under my hat." Taking off the white hat she wore to ride, Elly put it on Janie's head. "Then use this to get back behind the chutes. You can wish Mark and Jesse good luck for all of us."

Janie just stared at her.

"Go on," her best friend said, stepping out of the way so Janie could climb to the door of the box. "You know you want to see them before they ride. Shoo!"

"My mom—" Looking around, she found Abby

talking to Nicki about…something. Nicki glanced at Janie, and waved her on. "Go," she mouthed.

Helplessly snared in good intentions, Janie did what she was told.

JESSE HAD WATCHED ELLY'S RIDE from the rails of the bucking chutes. He'd winced at the extra two hundredths of a second between hers and the fastest time. Patting her on the back, he'd said, "Next year, honey. You'll be back next year."

Now he stood waiting for his own ride. After nine bulls for each of them, Mark still held first place, with Jesse in second and Sandy Thorpe in third. The scores were close enough that a spectacular ride for any one of them could win the title.

As the arena surface was smoothed one more time, though, Jesse's mind wasn't on the bull he'd be riding. He knew Janie would be in the audience, waiting to watch Mark. She'd attended every round of the Finals, yet somehow managed to slip away each night before he got so much as a glimpse of her. If they didn't talk tonight, he'd have to wait until everybody got settled back at home. Hell, it might be Christmas before he could make things right between them.

The chute gate creaked and clanged open. Rider Number Fifteen jumped out, on Tumble Dry. The bull took three spins and dropped the cowboy flat in the dirt.

One down, fourteen to go. These bulls were the best in the country—not even the best cowboys stayed on all the time.

Rider Ten took a horn through the thigh from Stick It To 'Em. Competition stopped while the medics carried him out.

After Number Eight, the announcer told the crowd that Ten would be okay. "Just sore for a while."

"Who here isn't?" Jesse asked of nobody in particular.

With Number Six in the chute, he went to the locker room for his rope and gloves. Sandy was there, sitting on the floor with a headset on and his eyes closed, listening to the music he insisted put his mind in the right place for a ride.

Mark sat on the bench nearest the chutes. He stood and offered Jesse a hand. "Good luck. Stay safe."

"You, too. I'll—"

But Mark was looking over Jesse's shoulder now, his brown eyes wide. "I don't believe it," he declared. "What are you doing here?" As he brushed past, Jesse jerked around.

"Janie!" Mark had his arms around her, picking her up off the floor. "Good to see you, girl."

"Thorpe, on deck!" they called from the chute. "Cody, next."

Sandy ambled toward the chutes, and Jesse punched him lightly in the shoulder. "Stick it," he ordered.

Mark offered Thorpe a handshake. "Good luck."

Sandy gave them both his lopsided grin and went out looking as though he had nothing more strenuous planned than a walk in the park. Jesse wished he felt half that calm. He had a bull to ride. A championship to win.

And having Janie standing five feet away was not helping his concentration.

Mark was holding her hands in his, talking fast. "How's Mom doing?"

Janie grinned. "She's great. Anxious to see you ride. Nicki's with her."

Her brother nodded. "Thanks for coming, Janie. For being here. For standing behind me all the way."

"I love you," she said softly. "You're my brother. We'll always be family."

Jesse figured he'd heard everything he needed to know. So he turned and headed down the hallway to the arena, prepared to meet his destiny.

Less than fifteen minutes later, a new world champion won the National Finals Rodeo bull riding competition.

THE ANNUAL CODY RODEO PARTY had been in full swing for more than an hour when the family's bull riders appeared at the entrance to the ballroom.

A roar went through the crowd. Dusty Cody approached the men and gave each of them a frothing bottle of champagne. Grinning, Mark took a swig and then pulled Nicki into his arms.

"I'm number two, but I try harder," he told her and gave his wife a hearty kiss.

Then he turned to Janie. "And one more for you, little sister."

Blinking back tears, Janie returned the hug. "Now go celebrate," she ordered Mark. "You deserve it."

Not far away, Jesse stood holding the bottle Dusty had given him. He wasn't drinking, and he wasn't smiling. But he was looking straight at her.

She couldn't avoid saying something, so she dodged the people between them and came up beside him. "You rode great. You should have scored higher."

Jesse shrugged. "Sandy deserved to win. He's been a finalist three times before this, and he's a hardworking cowboy. I'm glad he got his reward."

"There's always next year," she offered. A lame comment if ever she'd made one.

"We've already talked about that." He looked down at the bottle in his hand, frowning as if he didn't know how it got there or what to do with it.

Janie took the bottle, walked to a tray of used glasses along the wall and left it there, but then hesitated to return to Jesse. He had other people to greet.

She had a life to get on with.

But when she didn't come back, he joined her. "Can we talk?"

"We are talking." Her feeble smile didn't improve the joke.

"Alone."

"Jesse…" She blew out a sigh. "That's not necessary."

"It is if I ever plan to get a good night's sleep again."

Staring at his face, she saw the shadows circling his eyes, the lack of color under his tan. "Okay. We'll talk."

"Thanks." He glanced at the party around them and shook his head. "I can't leave right now. Want to meet me in the hotel library at midnight?"

She widened her eyes in surprise. "There's a library?"

"Yeah, on the second level. I figure it's the one place nobody in the whole hotel will be visiting at midnight on a Friday night."

Janie left the Cody party shortly after she'd talked to him—she'd only stopped in to be polite and to congratulate Mark. Returning to her room, she spent the hour staring at her textbook, but she didn't take in much about genetics. Her brain could only focus on what Jesse might want to say. She had a feeling she shouldn't expect to get any wishes granted or dreams fulfilled tonight.

At twelve o'clock, she stepped onto the elevator hoping for a solo ride. Instead, she found two cowboys propped up against the walls, both smelling of tequila and lime.

"Well, hello there." The short black-haired one gave her a white-toothed grin. "Aren't you a cowboy's dream?"

"More like a nightmare," she told him, staying toward the front of the car. "My ex-boyfriend will provide references."

"Aw, now, a cute little lady like you wouldn't hurt a fly," the redheaded guy said, standing up straighter.

"Depends on the fly," Janie told him.

The cowboys laughed. "Why don't you tell us all about it," Red suggested. "We'll treat you to as many drinks as it takes to…uh…finish the story."

"Yeah. We got a room down the road," added Blackie. "We'd be glad to offer you our hopi-hopitalty."

"Thanks, but my mom's sick. I'm just going down to buy her some aspirin."

Blackie snorted. "Sure. And I'm taking hay to my horse. He's stabled in the basement." He stepped closer, flanked by the redhead. Janie backed up until her heels touched the elevator doors.

"I'm not into nightlife," she told them, keeping her voice cool. If they touched her, she would have to hurt them. Somehow.

Blackie leaned in, pressing one hand against the door above her head. "You're in Vegas for a good time, right, honey?" Those bright white teeth came close and she could smell his sour breath. "So why not let us show you what you've been missing?"

Red, on her right, let his fingers do the walking—straight up her bare arm and along her shoulder, then down toward her cleavage.

In the next instant, Janie jerked her knee up and plowed her boot into Blackie's groin.

He gasped, backed up and bent over.

"Hey, bitch," Red growled, grabbing her arm. "You listen to me—"

At that moment, the elevator bell rang and the doors behind her slid open.

Janie backed up again…straight into a solid wall of muscle.

"What the hell?" Jesse demanded, right behind her. He sized up the situation in a flash. With the next breath, Janie found herself out of the elevator, maneuvered to the side.

"Excuse me for a minute," he said, then punched Red right in the nose.

The guy fell back into the elevator beside his friend on the floor, who was still groaning.

"That's what I do to flies," Janie told them, as Jesse retreated to stand beside her. "Have a good night." The elevator doors slid shut with a quiet click.

Jesse immediately set his hands on her shoulders and turned her to face him. His worried gaze moved over her from head to toes. "Are you okay?"

Janie's laugh was only slightly shaky. "Sure. They were just a couple of goons." She took in a deep breath, finally able to relax. "But thanks for the help. That second one was a little on the tall side. And the same trick wouldn't work twice."

"I suspect you would have figured something out." His hands tightened for a second, then released her. "The library is this way." He ushered her toward an inconspicuous door. Inside, shelves lined the walls behind armchairs and sofas of tufted leather. Brass lamps on dark wood tables didn't do much to break up the shadows.

"It really is a library." Janie walked around, checking out the shelves as a way of gaining time and space. "With books and everything."

Arms folded across his chest, Jesse leaned back against the door he'd closed behind him. "I discovered it one night when I was wandering around at 4:00 a.m. I'm only surprised there's not a slot machine in here somewhere."

She smiled at his joke and finally stopped wandering when she found she'd reached the farthest point of the room from where he stood. Taking a deep breath, she faced him.

"So, what did you want to talk about?"

He gave a brief chuckle. "You always do come right to the point, don't you?"

Janie shrugged, waiting for him to continue.

"I want to apologize," Jesse said. "For what happened at the jazz club."

She'd been afraid of that. "I don't need an apology. Anything else?"

"Yes, dammit." He glared at her. "Why are you making this so hard?"

Because it hurts so much. "Jesse, we're both adults. I enjoyed kissing you, but it's not that big a deal. Let's just forget it, go home and get back to real life."

"If it's not such a big deal, why have you spent the last week hiding?"

"I had studying to do. I've got a final in genetics in just over a week."

"That's an excuse. You were avoiding me. Along with the rest of my family."

"Look, Jesse, I know Mom and I were invited because of Mark. I never intended to intrude on your family, and I never thought you had to take me anywhere. There's a big gap between Codys—" she held one flattened hand up above her head and the other as low as she could "—and Hansens. You don't have to feel guilty, and you don't have to worry that I'll expect attention or—or anything once we get back to Markton. So just let it go." She tried out a grin. "Remember the rule—What happens in Vegas, stays in Vegas."

Jesse muttered a rude word. "You're making it so easy. Am I supposed to thank you?"

"Not necessary."

"Great. So, like the arrogant, selfish SOB of a Cody that I am, I can just treat you like dirt and walk away without a backward glance?"

"I'm saying that's not what happened. Don't beat yourself up."

"And how I felt about holding you, kissing you, connecting with you—that's irrelevant? Or are you just assuming that because I'm a Cody, you wouldn't expect anything like real emotions from me?"

"You're the one who said it was a mistake."

"You never let me explain why."

"I didn't have to." She met his glare with one of her own. "We don't belong together, for reasons that are complicated and not our fault, but still valid. I've got places to go—vet school in Colorado, I hope. You've got a big job on the Cottonwood Ranch and more work than you can handle. My mother's sick. Your parents are getting older." She took a deep breath and blew it out again. "Then there's Mark. I know you don't like him, and that's hard for me to take. He'll always be in the way. Tell me what I've forgotten."

The fire in Jesse's eyes had gone out. He dropped his chin and stared at the floor, his shoulders losing their straight line.

"I guess that covers it," he said in a tired voice. "I guess I wasted your time, coming here. Not to mention getting you into trouble."

"You wouldn't be the man I l—" She swallowed the first word that came to mind. "You wouldn't be the man I like if this didn't matter to you, Jesse. Thanks for caring. I won't forget the good times we've had together in Las Vegas."

His lips curved, but she wouldn't call the result a smile. "Me, neither. I'll walk you back to your room."

He held the door open for her to leave the library, and waited beside her without speaking until the elevator arrived. Once the doors closed, he pushed the button and stepped to the side, putting as much space between them as possible, digging his hands into his pockets.

"Let me know when you want to fly home," he said, watching the floor numbers on the digital display. "Since I didn't win, I have no more real commitments. I just need a morning to get the plane ready to go."

"Um…I bought tickets for Mom and me," Janie said. "We'll be leaving early tomorrow morning."

Jesse turned toward her, an expression of outrage and hurt on his face. He opened his mouth, paused and shut it again.

"Okay," he said in a ragged voice. "If that's what works best for you."

With perfect timing, the elevator doors opened at that moment onto the fortieth floor. Janie stepped out and turned back to watch Jesse exit.

"Thanks for everything." She held out a hand, thinking maybe they could part with a friendly handshake. Maybe she could touch him one more time.

But Jesse kept his hands hidden. "You're welcome. The pleasure was all mine." His blue eyes met hers for a second, then slid away. "See you around sometime, Janie. Take care."

Just like that, he turned on his heel and walked down the hall toward the Cody suite, leaving her standing with her hand stuck out in the air. Untouched.

"Bye, Jesse," she whispered. "It's been good loving you."

Chapter Seven

Jesse seldom favored lost causes. His dad had drummed the facts of life into his head since he was old enough to walk—ranching required a man to be practical, to analyze profits versus losses and be sure he came out on the high end of a deal. During the past eight years under Jesse's supervision, the Cody family cattle operation had made money every quarter. He prided himself on being dependable that way.

Yet here he stood in the aisle of the Markton Feed and Grain Store, staring blindly at a shelf of horse wormers he didn't need and waiting for the chance to make a complete fool of himself by asking for a favor when he already knew the answer would be "no."

Not just "no," he figured, but "no chance in hell." Janie did have a forthright way of speaking her mind.

He wouldn't blame her for turning him down. Things between them certainly hadn't ended on a good note last weekend. What possible reason would she have for wanting to help him out? Why had he even bothered to come?

Avoiding the answer to that question, Jesse headed for the exit—just as the quick tap of boot heels on concrete announced Janie's approach.

"Well, if it isn't Jesse Cody." Hearing her light voice set up a wave of…something…inside of him. "What brings you into town at 10:00 a.m. on a workday?"

He swallowed hard, then took off his hat as he turned to face his fate. "Hey, Janie." He started to follow up with the usual, "How's it going?" but the words re-arranged themselves without his will. "You're looking pretty this morning."

And she was, with her hair woven into a shiny black braid falling over her shoulder, showing off her slender throat and cute, pointed chin. The red shirt tucked into faded jeans displayed the sexy curves of her waist and hips.

Her dark brown eyes glinted at him, though she didn't actually smile. "Don't look so surprised," she told him. "Everybody has a good hair day now and then. Even me."

He frowned and shook his head. "That's not what I meant to say."

She crossed her arms over her breasts. "Oh…so I'm not looking pretty after all?"

"No, I—" His brain had melted to mush. Holding up a hand, Jesse took a second to rebuild it. "You look fine. You always do. But I came in to ask…that is, I wanted to see if—" How could someone who barely came up to his shoulder be so intimidating?

Janie leaned her shoulder against the end of the shelf, as if preparing to wait all day. "If…?"

He cleared his throat. Maybe he should start with the facts. "When I got home Monday afternoon, I realized Sundae, my gelding, was lame. Dr. Bill confirmed he's got a bowed tendon." He nodded when Janie winced. "Yeah. Doc says it'll be a long recovery." Jesse took a deep breath and began the hard part. "Elly suggested maybe you could help."

He'd rushed the words, but Janie obviously understood him, because she straightened up and let her hands drop to her sides. "Me? What could I do?"

Jesse attempted to backtrack. "Well, Sundae will need hand-walking a couple of times a day." Janie opened her mouth and he went on before she could speak. "I know—I could get one of the hands to take care of it."

"I seem to recall you do have a couple of guys working for you out there on that big old ranch of yours."

"Sure." He ran a hand over his hair. "But they're not always careful. One of them put Rowdy into the same field with Sundae, which is how we ended up in this predicament to begin with. Rowdy chases Sundae every time they're within striking distance."

"I guess that guy is looking for a new job this week?"

Jesse shrugged. "Anyway—"

But she put up a hand to stop him. "Anyway, I am not one of your employees, Jesse Cody. And you could walk the horse yourself."

He huffed a breath. "I could. At 5:00 a.m., in the dark, before I head out on a full day's roundup, maybe. And then again when I get back, in the dark, at 8:00 or 9:00 p.m."

"Too bad for you." She shook her head. "Wish I could help you out, but between home and school and work—not to mention the time I put in at Dr. Bill's—I've got all I can handle. I can't afford to hire somebody to take care of my life just so I can walk your horse." With a quick turn, she headed away from him, toward the back of the store.

"Janie—" He grabbed her wrist before she got too

far out of reach. He had to convince her, for Sundae's sake. "Elly says you're a healer."

She pivoted slowly back to face him. "What are you talking about? What did she tell you?"

"That you're good with animals. Dr. Bill depends on you for his emergency backup."

Pulling her arm free of his hold, she waved away his evasion. "That's not what you said a second ago."

Jesse moved closer and lowered his voice. "Elly told me you have a—a gift. Animals get better, faster, when you touch and talk to them, work with them."

Janie looked down at the floor. "Your sister has a big mouth."

"Is it true? You never mentioned it." Staring down at her, he noticed again the straight line where her black bangs fell forward from the rest of her shiny hair. The weave of her braid caught his attention, and then the vulnerable nape of her neck—smooth skin with a small, kissable mole slightly off-center to the right. He knew exactly how her hair would smell, if he leaned close, if he kissed her...

Man, was he a mess.

He jerked his mind onto the right track. "Could you heal Sundae?"

"I'm not a vet. Yet."

Jesse heard the longing in her voice. "Elly says you're better than a vet."

Janie snorted and shook her head. "That's ridiculous."

"Look." Jesse set one hand on her shoulder and lifted her chin up with the other so he could see her eyes. "I don't have to explain to you the partnership that develops over the years between horse and rider. I'm sure you know exactly how much I depend on Sundae, and how much I care about him."

He squeezed his own eyes shut for a second, then fixed his gaze on hers again. "Right now Sundae is standing in a stall, miserable and bored. Dr. Bill isn't sure he'll ever be fit to work again, and that makes me miserable. I've got a hundred other horses I can ride, but none I trust like Sundae. So I'll do, and try, anything to get him back to work. Can you help me?"

She took a step backward, escaping his hold with something very close to a shudder. "I'll have to think about it," she said, tucking her fingers into the front pockets of her jeans. "As soon as I decide, I'll give you a call."

With his mouth half-open to try more persuasion, Jesse decided to ease the pressure. She hadn't outright refused again—that was better than he'd hoped for. Like a frisky filly, if he pushed too hard, she might get riled up and say no, for good.

So he snapped his jaw shut and swallowed the protest. "Thanks, Janie. I'll be waiting to hear from you."

Then, before he could ruin Sundae's chances, he shoved his hat onto his head and marched toward the door. He'd made his case, which was what he'd come here to do.

He could only hope Janie's kind heart would meet him halfway.

Janie stood where she was, staring, as Jesse's long strides took him to the store exit. She didn't draw a breath until the door thudded shut behind him.

Then she filled her lungs to capacity and blew the air out again in a big rush. Along with oxygen she caught the scent of his aftershave—the same scent he'd worn to the concert in Vegas, the same one he'd been using since he first picked up a razor. Once, when she was sixteen, she'd bought a bottle for herself and sprinkled it on her pillow to pretend he'd laid his head there. She'd had some sweetly sexy dreams before wash day came around again.

Those dreams were nothing compared to the reality she'd known, the heat and heaven of kissing Jesse Cody.

But this time, she intended to stop dreaming. After all these years, she was determined to let him go.

Janie whipped around and headed for the store's office, where Ruth Pearsoll sat sorting receipts. "I hate him," she told the older woman, dropping into the chair beside the desk.

"Who's that, honey?" Ruth didn't look up from her slips of paper. She and her husband, Leslie, owned the Markton Feed and Grain Store, where Ruth managed the office.

"Jesse Cody."

She'd confided some of the events in Vegas to Ruth, so the older woman understood part of the problem, at least. "What has he done now?" A kind and gentle woman, Ruth had been Janie's refuge since she started working at the feed store during high school.

"He wants me to rehabilitate his hurt horse."

"Ah. Did you agree?"

"I told him I'd think about it. And call him."

"Then you can call him back and refuse." The older woman continued with her filing. "If you want to be done with him, then be done. Just say no."

Janie heard the words, but she couldn't seem to incorporate the concept into her brain. "I might be able to help the horse. I've got a special rub, made with bee poison, that's good for torn tendons."

"I know, honey, but you have to think about yourself. You told me you and Jesse just don't match up."

"Well, it's not so much the two of us as all the stuff going on with our families."

"Mmm." Ruth opened a drawer in the desk and began rifling through it.

"There's the situation with Mark, you know. What's going to happen to Jesse if Mark steps in as the oldest Cody son?"

"Yes, that is a problem."

"And while his mother was very nice while we were in Vegas, you know she won't like having her son date Abby Hansen's daughter."

"Possibly. Although she's always been glad to have you as Elly's friend."

"That's not the same, is it?"

Ruth looked up from the drawer, with a faraway expression on her face. "I suppose not. My Troy never got real serious about a girl, but I can imagine that finding out her mother had seduced my Leslie might color my reaction." Ruth and Leslie had lost their son Troy in a rodeo accident.

Janie nodded. "And it's not like I'm ever going to be on the same social level with the Codys. I've always been Elly's connection to the poor side of town."

Ruth clicked her tongue. "I'm not sure that matters to anyone but you, Janie."

"Oh, it would matter to his parents, I'm sure." She propped her chin on her hand and sat thinking…sulking, in fact.

"So tell Jesse you can't help the horse and move on."

"Right. That's what I should do." Beyond the office

doorway, the bell on the store door jangled, signaling a customer. Before Janie could take a breath, the sound repeated. She got to her feet with a groan. "Business is picking up. I'd better get to work."

Ruth crossed the room to give her a one-armed hug. "When you go out to the Cottonwood Ranch, be sure to make him pay you for your time. That'll be one way to keep yourself on an equal footing, and at a distance. Don't worry, the Codys can afford it."

Janie stared at Ruth with her mouth open. "But I didn't—"

Her friend smiled. "I knew from the first you'd be going. You could never resist helping an injured horse. Just be careful and don't get hurt, yourself."

Just how she was supposed to follow that advice, given that she'd probably be seeing Jesse nearly every day, Janie couldn't begin to imagine.

AFTER TWO HOURS driving a truck and trailer and five hours on horseback herding cattle, Jesse and his crew returned to the barns to end their workday. The horses had to be unsaddled, brushed down and fed before the men could get to their own dinners. Jesse still had paperwork to do.

First, though, he walked through the stallion barn to visit Sundae. The only light came from the red exit signs above the doors at either end of the long aisle. From the shadowed stalls came the crunch of hay being chewed or the rustle of bedding as horses shifted position. A nicker greeted Jesse now and then as he approached some of his favorites and he always stopped to stroke a cheek, a nose or a glossy neck.

Sundae had been put into a stall next to the door, so he could at least see outside through the big windows.

With the clink of his spurs to announce him, Jesse expected to see his horse's brown head with its white blaze poked over the top of the stall door in welcome. From the aisle, however, Sundae's stall looked empty.

Jesse stepped up to the door. "Sundae? You okay, boy?"

The pinto stood against the far wall, head hanging to his knees.

With shaking hands, Jesse fumbled the door latch open. "Hey, bud, what's wro—"

A pale face appeared near the horse's head. "Jesse, it's me. Janie."

"What the hell are you doing down there?" Worry added an edge to his voice.

"What you asked me to," she shot back at him, in the same tone. Somehow, the shadows at the back of the stall resolved into his horse and a woman standing beside him, stroking his withers. "I called, but Doris said you'd gone on a roundup and wouldn't be back until late. So I thought I'd come on over and get started anyway."

Jesse propped his hands on his hips. He still couldn't get his heart rate down, though not necessarily because of worry over the horse. "In the dark?"

"I don't need the light."

"Well, I do." Backing up, he flipped on the overhead lamp for the stall. "What is it you're doing, exactly?"

She hesitated for a long moment, mouth open as if to say something. With a shake of her head, though, Janie simply turned back to the horse.

"I'm rubbing his legs." As her hand traveled across Sundae's shoulder, down his foreleg and over his knee, she gradually knelt in the shavings on the floor. Using both hands, one after the other, she caressed Sundae's injured leg. "It's an old racing technique. The grooms would spend a big part of their day rubbing their horse's legs, trying to decrease inflammation."

Picking up a bottle on the floor nearby, Janie squirted liquid into both her palms before continuing her massage. "This is a menthol-alcohol blend. Good for reducing swelling."

"And you think that will help heal the ligament?" He wasn't sure what he'd expected, but simple massage seemed too easy.

"Can't hurt." She didn't look up. "I'm going to be here for at least another half hour. You can stay if you want to, but this is as exciting as it gets."

That sounded to him like a suggestion to leave. "I've got some paperwork to finish in my office. Over in the cow barn," he clarified, since she'd probably never noticed where he worked.

"I know where your office is, Jesse." She flashed him a tolerant glance. "Elly and I used to run all over this place. I probably know about rooms you've never noticed."

"Doubtful." He couldn't repress a grin. "But that was a long time ago. I haven't seen you around the ranch for…I don't know, maybe years."

"Most definitely years." She squirted alcohol on her hands again. "Elly and I meet for lunch or dinner now, like the adults we're supposed to be. Weekends, sometimes." Her smile faded. "We used to, anyway. William takes up most of her time these days."

"We miss her around here, too. I guess that's what romance does, though—breaks up families."

"And makes new ones."

His mind immediately went to his dad, and he spoke without thinking. "Unless there's already a spouse in the picture."

Janie's hands went still. In the next instant, she jumped to her feet, gathered the bottle and a knapsack nearby and stomped into the aisle.

"I knew my first instinct was the right one," she said hotly. "I should have listened to my gut and stayed home."

Jesse latched the stall door behind him, then lengthened his strides until he caught up with her. "I didn't intend to insult you, Janie. I didn't mean to say that out loud."

"Don't apologize. I'd rather hear what you're thinking." She pushed through the exterior door leading to the walkway between the horse and cattle barns, letting the panel swing back into his face. "And now I have, I know where I don't belong."

Dodging the door, Jesse lunged forward and got his hand around her elbow, then dug in his heels and brought them both to a stop.

"Don't go," he pleaded through gritted teeth. "Please."

Her bones felt small and light against his palm.

"Give me one good reason." She didn't look back at him.

Only one reason stood a chance in hell of working. "Sundae needs all the help he can get."

"So he can go back to carrying you around?"

"Yeah." He grinned, though she wasn't looking. "But I'm not as hard on my horses as I am on my employees."

"Lucky horses." She drew in a deep breath and blew it out again. "You know you're paying me to do this? Thirty dollars an hour?"

"Whatever you want. Just take care of Sundae."

"Okay." She turned her head, finally, to look down at his hand around her arm. "Excuse me."

He released her and stepped back, ignoring a surge of reluctance. "Were you finished?"

"No, as a matter of fact, I'd just started. I wanted to do all four legs. When one leg is injured, especially a front leg, the other three take on extra strain."

The tension in Jesse's neck eased. "If you'll go back to Sundae, I promise I won't bother you again." That would be better for both of them. "Like I said, I've got paperwork to catch up on. Just stop by and let me know you're leaving."

"Yes, boss." Walking quickly, she headed back to the horse barn with a swing to her hips Jesse enjoyed watching until the closing door blocked his view.

JANIE DIDN'T BREATHE UNTIL she reached Sundae's stall again. Once she was sure she wasn't being followed, she leaned limply against the wall and worked to recover from the roller coaster ride of meeting up with Jesse.

She should have called out when she'd heard him coming down the aisle toward the stall, so she could forgive his burst of temper at being surprised. But the spouse comment had fired her temper.

Of course, he'd also proved her point. They would never get past what had happened between his father and her mother. Any relationship between them was doomed before either of them was even born, a fact they both needed to remember.

But Jesse had come after her, had actually touched her—grabbed her arm—to keep her from leaving. She'd felt the pressure of each of his fingers separately, and a circle of warmth where his palm had rested. That was the point at which her good sense blew away with the

GET 2 BOOKS

We'd like to send you two *Harlequin American Romance®* novels absolutely free.
Accepting them puts you under no obligation to purchase any more books.

HOW TO GET YOUR
2 FREE BOOKS AND 2 FREE GIFTS

1. Return the reply card today, and we'll send you two *Harlequin American Romance* novels, absolutely free! We'll even pay the postage!

2. Accepting free books places you under no obligation to buy anything, ever. Whatever you decide, the free books and gifts are yours to keep, free!

3. We hope that after receiving your free books you'll want to remain a subscriber, but the choice is yours—to continue or cancel, any time at all!

EXTRA BONUS

You'll also get two free mystery gifts! (worth about $10)

FREE!

BUSINESS REPLY MAIL

FIRST-CLASS MAIL   PERMIT NO. 717   BUFFALO, NY

POSTAGE WILL BE PAID BY ADDRESSEE

THE READER SERVICE
PO BOX 1867
BUFFALO NY 14240-9952

NO POSTAGE
NECESSARY
IF MAILED
IN THE
UNITED STATES

wind and her breathing got all shaky. Instead of saving herself, she'd agreed to stay.

That didn't mean she had to sit around sighing, like the lovesick schoolgirl she used to be. No, she'd decided to move on in her life, to investigate new opportunities and wider horizons. That's why, with her genetics final out of the way, she'd entered a charity rodeo this weekend, up in Montana. She doubted she'd win, because she and her horse, Chica, hadn't practiced much since Thanksgiving.

But the feed store was only open until noon on Saturdays in December, so Ruth Pearsoll had approved her Saturday off. Mark and Nicki would be watching her mother and Elly had promised to give Sundae his twice-a-day walks. Janie looked forward to getting away from Cody, and the Codys, especially Jesse. The rodeo raised funds to provide Christmas for underprivileged kids, yet another good reason to make the effort.

Settling on her knees beside Sundae, she squirted alcohol into her hands and began rubbing his right hind leg with gentle downward strokes. She usually found rubbing legs as soothing as the horse did. Tonight, however, she couldn't release the tension in her chest and shoulders and neck. Jesse's presence complicated her thoughts and stirred up emotions she tried to keep under control.

When she finished with Sundae's legs, she spent time stroking the gelding's neck and shoulders while murmuring some of the Lakota songs she had learned from her grandmother. She prayed for balance to be restored in Sundae's world…and in Jesse's. She thought he probably needed that even more than his favorite horse did.

Outside the stall once again, she pulled on her jacket

and picked up her supply satchel to walk through the nearly silent stallion barn. The size and scope of the Cody facilities amazed everyone who visited. In addition to the ten-stall stallion barn and a thirty-stall building designed to house mares in the Cody quarter horse breeding program—Anne Cody's pet project—Jesse worked on the beef cattle operation in the equally huge cow barn, where J. W. Cody also pursued the development of prize-winning rodeo bulls.

Janie frowned as she pushed open the door into the cow barn. From what Mark had said when they'd had a chance to talk in Vegas, his goal was to have a place of his own and to make a name for himself breeding bulls, just like J. W. Cody. Was the similarity coincidence? Heredity? Or had Mark made the choice because he knew he could get Cody assistance?

She hadn't asked her brother that question. Chances were good if she did, he'd just scowl and walk out on her. He was a happy man, now that he'd found love with Nicki. But he'd never confided much in Janie, and he wasn't about to start. Maybe he'd always felt he was different. Maybe he'd known somewhere deep inside that he was a Cody even before her mother told him the truth.

As she turned the corner into the aisle leading to the parking lot, Janie saw a triangle of light emerging from a doorway about halfway down on the left. Jesse had said he'd be working—surely he wasn't still here at 10:00 p.m.?

In fact, he was still in his office, though not working. He was leaning back into the dark green leather of his big desk chair, head resting against the side and eyes closed. Soft, rumbly snores came through his open mouth.

Smiling, Janie watched him for a long minute. He had to be uncomfortable, yet he was sound asleep. Poor guy, he'd been telling the truth when he said he worked from dawn until late at night. He seemed so vulnerable, so harmless, dozing like this.

All at once, his hand jerked into the air and he shuddered, from his shoulders to his knees. Then he sat up, with his spine as stiff and straight as a lodgepole pine tree.

Whether she deserved it or not, Janie had a feeling she was in for the dressing-down of her life.

Chapter Eight

But Jesse's eyes never opened. In the next moment, he sank back into the chair, flopped his head to the left and resumed snoring.

Janie gradually released the breath she was holding and allowed her body to relax. What would she have said if he'd woken up and seen her gawking at him?

She didn't know, and she wasn't going to risk having to find out. Bracing herself, she took a step forward, put a hand forward and gave Jesse's shoulder a firm shake.

He didn't wake up, didn't even stir. Now she was stuck touching him, feeling the cord of muscle running along the back of his shoulder up into his neck, the arch of his collarbone and the hollow behind it. Her palm could almost sense the texture of the fair skin underneath his chambray shirt. Her eyes could happily spend forever studying his face, his silver-blond hair and thick eyelashes, his full, sensual lower lip.

But her mind could imagine how much worse she'd feel if he woke up and found her groping him in his sleep. So she shook him again, and again. "Jesse. Jesse, wake up." How tired he must be, to sleep so soundly!

Finally, she used both hands. "Come on, Jesse. You can't sleep here all night."

A grimace of pain contracted his face. "I'm plenty comfortable. Let me be."

Janie stepped back. In another minute, Jesse frowned even more violently, groaned and lifted heavy eyelids. "Janie? Is there a problem?"

"N-no." Except that he looked so damn sexy she could hardly speak. "I thought you should go to bed, that's all, instead of spending the night in your chair."

"Oh." His eyes closed again. "I do that a lot." Would he go back to sleep? At least he was still talking.

She'd done what she could. And she'd better get out of here before she did what she shouldn't. "Then I'll leave you to your rest." As she reached the door, though, she heard the chair squeak.

"No, you're right." When she turned around, he'd gotten to his feet and was shrugging into his heavy coat. "A bed would be better." He turned off the lamp and, with a few unsteady steps, joined her at the door.

They walked side by side, but without talking, toward the door to the parking lot. The exit sign was once again their only source of light and Janie's unruly mind headed straight down the wrong path—Jesse's arms going around her, Jesse's mouth capturing hers...

But he pushed the heavy door open without touching her and she stepped outside into the cold, black night.

Jesse waved a hand as he headed toward his truck. "Thanks for saving me a stiff neck."

"No problem." She couldn't help asking, "Did you get dinner?"

He rubbed his hand over his hair. "Uh...no. I'll grab something before I go to bed."

Janie would have offered to make him some food, but

she stopped herself just in time. She couldn't be Jesse's caretaker, no matter how much she wanted the job.

"See you around," she said instead.

She drove her cold truck home, said good-night to the woman who had stayed extra hours with her mom and ate her own cold dinner alone in front of the TV. Maybe Jesse wasn't the only one who needed to be taken care of?

Then maybe they were both just plain out of luck.

To HER RELIEF AS WELL as disappointment, Janie didn't see Jesse at the barn on Thursday morning—the team had left for their roundup two hours before she arrived at seven-thirty. She gave Sundae his leg rub, plus a short walk outside the stall, then dashed back to Markton to hold down the register at the store. On her lunch break, she hurried home to check on her mom.

As she turned down the unpaved road leading to the five hardscrabble acres the Hansens called home, Janie observed her background unsentimentally. This wasn't the Codys' Cottonwood Ranch, with grassy rolling hills, pine trees and cottonwoods standing against a backdrop of the Rocky Mountains and the flashing waters of the Shoshone River.

The prefab home she'd always lived in sat on the same flat plain as the rest of Markton, exposed to the wind, sun and, most of all, dust. No manicured lawn, no fancy gate, no driveway—just a metal box set down in front of four acres of fenced rangeland where she kept her barrel racing horse. Chica's shed looked to be in better condition than the house itself.

Mark did his best to help with maintenance, but most of his winnings and his time went straight back into his rodeo career. Her feed store earnings paid the house bills—there weren't too many—and she and Mark managed to cover medical expenses together. Of course, the prize money from placing second at NFR would help, but he and Nicki would want to buy their own place and start their life together soon. So they didn't have cash left over for cosmetic details on a thirty-year-old trailer.

Inside the house wasn't quite so grim. Bright, wool blankets hid the worn upholstery in the living room, and flowered curtains softened the windows. Abby Hansen had always kept a clean house, and Janie did her best to follow her mother's example. As she walked by the sofa, she straightened the magazines on the coffee table and noted the dust on the TV cabinet for wiping off later. In the kitchen, she ran hot water and squirted dish soap into one side of the double sink to deal with the bowls and cups from breakfast.

"Mom?" Drying her hands on a towel, she walked down the narrow hall. "Hey, Mom? Want some lunch?"

At the door to her mother's room, she sagged a little against the frame as she saw Abby still lying in bed, just as she had been when Janie left at seven. Not asleep, now or then—Abby's wide, frightened eyes had been easy to see even in the predawn dark.

Janie sat down on the edge of the mattress and smoothed back her mother's graying hair. "Hey, Mom. How about getting up for a little bit? Maybe a shower? Fresh clothes?"

Shaking her head, Abby rolled farther toward the wall. Since the flight home from Las Vegas, her condition had taken a rapid turn for the worse. Their week together seemed more and more like a wistful dream.

Janie put a hand on the thin shoulder she could reach. "Now, Mom, you can't stay here all afternoon. I've got to go back to work. Let me help you get cleaned up. You'll feel better about everything. I know you will."

Coaxing, reassuring, pleading, Janie at last convinced her mother to leave the bed and take a shower. After helping with the process, Janie combed Abby's waist-length hair then wove it into a smooth braid. Just as she helped her mom into a clean dress, the front door of the house opened and closed.

"Anybody home?" Mark's quiet voice somehow penetrated the whole house.

Abby stood up straighter, and she smiled. "I'm coming." She turned to Janie and put a hand to her cheek. "Thank you, so much. What would I do without you?"

"That's not something we have to worry about." Janie blinked away tears as she led her mother back toward the kitchen.

Mark stood peering into the refrigerator. "What do we have to eat? I'm starved."

"Get out of the way, cowboy." Janie pushed him playfully backward and took his place. "Go sit down with Mom a few minutes and I'll warm up some food."

"Thanks." Reaching past her, he grabbed a can of soda off the shelf, then went to join Abby on the sofa. In answer to her questions, he told her—for maybe the hundredth time—that he had married a really wonderful girl and he'd come in second at the National Finals Rodeo. For the hundredth time, Abby was surprised and delighted to hear she had a daughter-in-law.

"Are you going to live here?" she asked as they sat down at the table with leftover meatloaf and mashed potatoes. "I can move into the small room and you and—and—"

"Nicki," Mark inserted gently.

"You and Nicki could have my big room." She smashed her fork through the food without actually eating any of it.

"Thanks, Mom." He patted her hand. "Right now, we're staying with Nicki's dad. He's got plenty of room."

Janie put her fingers on Abby's wrist. "Take a bite, Mom. You should eat."

Her mother dropped the fork onto the plate. "I'm not hungry." She looked at Mark again. "What can I do for you? What kind of plans do you have?"

Mark managed to deflect the question, assuring Abby he and Nicki would let her know what they needed. He took a turn urging her to eat and, for her son, Abby managed to swallow a few bites.

Then she yawned. "I'm so tired. I think I need to lie down on my bed a little while."

Once her mother had crawled back into bed and fallen asleep, Janie returned to the kitchen where Mark had brewed a pot of coffee and was pouring himself a cup. "Want one?"

"Yeah." Once more seated in her chair at the table, she mostly played with her own food. "What brings you over for lunch?"

He leaned the chair back on two legs and took a swig from his coffee. "Just felt like I should be here."

Janie nodded. "I know what you mean. I could tell even in the dark this morning that this wasn't a good day."

Mark cocked an eyebrow. "Since when does the feed store open in the dark?"

She swore to herself as she realized what she'd said. "I—I had a horse to work with first. An injured horse."

Mark's chair legs thudded against the vinyl floor. "Whose horse?"

"Jesse's." She didn't bother to lie. He'd find out eventually.

"Dammit, Janie. Why the hell would you do a thing like that?"

"Like what? Help an injured horse?"

"Work for Jesse Cody."

"You're a member of the family. What's the problem with me working for your brother?"

Mark glared at her for a long moment. "I know you're not that dumb," he said. "First of all, Jesse hates my guts, now more than ever, after I beat him in the National Finals. My guess is he'll take that hate out on you if he gets a chance."

"Jesse's not like that."

He muttered a rude word. "Second, I'm a long way from being a part of the family. Things might have looked good in Vegas, but Anne is still an iceberg where I'm concerned. Those four brothers aren't too happy about what's happened, either, especially Jesse. I'm not sure you're safe anywhere on that spread."

"You're ridiculous. I've been friends with all of them for years, which is more than you can say. Nobody's going to hurt me."

In a swift move, he left his chair and moved next to her, at the same time capturing her hands in his. Then her brother looked her straight in the eye, his own dark gaze tender and concerned.

"Most of all," he said, "I'm afraid your feelings are gonna get you into trouble."

Janie turned her head. "I don't know what you're talking about."

"Yes, you do." He gave her hands a little shake. "I

worried about you in Vegas, but then you got smart and stayed away from him. Now you'll see him every day—"

"I won't." She got up and took her cup to the sink. "I didn't seen him this morning at all."

With her back turned, she heard him sigh. Then his hands closed over her shoulders.

"The Codys aren't like us, Janie. You know they want only the best of everything for their family. We're not in the same league."

"You're a Cody," she whispered, although her heart rejoiced to know he still thought of himself as a Hansen.

"I'm J.W.'s mistake," he said almost as quietly. His hands tightened, then he let her go and went into the living room. "Mom said she'd been by herself all morning. Did Mrs. Hillier not come?"

"I left early, so I didn't see her, but surely she would let us know if she couldn't be here. I'll call and find out." Alma Hillier usually stayed with Abby while Janie worked. She wasn't completely reliable, but she was the only resource Markton offered.

Mark stood by the door, fidgeting with the handle. "Mom's getting worse, isn't she?"

"Since we got back? Yeah."

He left without saying anything else. Janie hoped Nicki would be able to give him the comfort he needed.

If only somebody, somewhere, could do the same for her.

FRIDAY AFTERNOON, JESSE THREW his duffel bag and bull rigging into the backseat of his truck and headed for the High Country Christmas Rodeo in Gardiner,

Montana. All the proceeds from this show went to brighten the holidays for needy children, so he'd made a point of being there every year since he'd joined the professional rodeo circuit. If he won—and he'd won more of these shows than he'd lost—he contributed his own winnings to the charity.

He bought gas in Cody, then headed north, bypassing the mountains and Yellowstone Park. The three-hour drive through the park was a nice one, but the road closed in November due to snow at the higher elevations. Hard as it was to believe, Christmas Eve was just a week away.

Thoughts of snow reminded him of the night Janie had insisted on driving him home, not to mention their time together in Vegas. Of course, there were the nine nights of the Finals when she'd avoided him, and the one night she'd made it clear she wanted him to leave her alone.

He'd tried. Honestly. But his plan to keep away from her in the barn had failed totally—since Wednesday, he'd seen her at least once and sometimes twice a day. While he could take some of the blame, she certainly didn't make staying away any easier.

Somehow, everything she wore looked sexy these days. Every time they talked, he would see her mouth and remember her taste. Her hands, giving Sundae a rubdown, only made Jesse want the same for himself.

The situation was damn bad when a cowboy envied his horse.

Nonetheless, he was determined not to make a move that would bring Janie closer—a decision for which valid reasons existed. They agreed that no good could come from them being together. He didn't intend to change his mind.

Part of him, though—a rebellious, spoiled boy he tried to ignore—refused to keep quiet. Just because J.W. had once messed up his love life shouldn't make a difference to Jesse, thirty years later. Damn Mark, damn J.W. and anybody else who might object. The teenager in Jesse insisted he had a right to do whatever felt best between him and Janie Hansen.

By the time he reached Gardiner, he had a plan in place for the weekend. He'd ride his three bulls, then after the rodeo, he'd hit the bars and enjoy himself. His fellow cowboys would be there—he could shoot the breeze, maybe shoot some pool, do some dancing and find himself a buckle bunny to spend time with. When he got home Sunday night, he'd have smoothed out the kinks a certain black-haired woman had worked into his life.

His plan went to hell at nine-fifteen that evening.

He drew a mean one—Big Bad John—for his first ride, but stayed on until the buzzer, landing on his feet when he jumped off. The crowd roared their appreciation of his score. Jesse tipped his hat, then gave them a wave. As he scanned the stands, still grinning, his eyes focused on the one person he did not want to see tonight.

There, in the middle of the stands, stood Janie Hansen, looking as cute as a button in her bright red shirt.

JANIE SAW JESSE'S EYES WIDEN. He'd seen her, despite the big crowd. Judging by the way his grin faded, her presence wasn't a pleasant surprise.

The people around her were still standing and applauding but she sat down—hiding, she supposed.

Dee Ferris, the friend who'd come with her to Gardiner, joined her on the bleacher. "What's wrong?"

"Jesse saw me. He's not happy about it."

"Too bad for Jesse." Dee tossed her blond curls back behind her shoulders. "It's not like you're chasing him or anything."

"I didn't know he was riding until I got here."

"Right. Maybe he should've looked at the roster and seen that you're competing this weekend. And winning tonight, might we add?"

Janie grinned. "That was a good feeling."

"You're damn right it was. So kiss off Mr. High-and-Mighty Cody." Dee stood and pulled Janie up with her. "We're gonna enjoy ourselves in Montana. Do us some eatin' and some drinkin' and some dancin'!"

Dee jigged down the aisle, stepping on toes as she went, but she was so cute, most people grinned instead of getting mad. Especially the guys. Janie's pride noted that she got her own share of winks, and one pinch, as she followed.

Unfortunately, the only winks she wanted came from a certain pair of big, blue eyes. She didn't think she would change her mind no matter how much she ate, drank and danced. This weekend, though, she'd sworn to do her best.

Walking along the midway on their way to the truck, she couldn't help searching the throng for a familiar white hat. Janie wasn't sure if she would run away or toward that hat if she found it.

She and Dee were still within range of the announcer in the arena, though, when he called out the bull riding results.

"Our winner tonight—no surprise here, folks—is Jesse Cody with a seventy-eight-point ride. Let's give ol' Jesse a big hand! He's here every year with us at the High Country Christmas Rodeo, doing his best for a great cause by donating his winnings to the kids. Thanks, Jesse!"

"I didn't know he came up here every year." Dee stood outside the rented stall as Janie made sure her horse had everything she needed for the night.

"I probably should have." Janie gave Chica a final rub and closed the door, double-checking the bolt. "But the Codys are always traveling to different rodeos in different states. It's hard to keep track of who goes where. Mark doesn't come to this show because he'd feel bad keeping the money he won, even though he needs it. Now I guess I understand why, if Jesse donates his."

"That's a hard act to follow." Dee popped her gum as they got into the truck. "So, where do we feel like going? I hear the bars specialize in types of food— you've got pizzas at one place, ribs and burgers over here and Mexican over there. What do we feel like? The rib place has a dance floor and a band."

Janie pulled in a deep breath. She was going to do this thing and she was going to enjoy it. "I'm feeling like ribs."

"Good choice." Dee tuned the radio to a country station, turned the volume up and sang along to the cowboy song. Off key.

"I hope the band sounds better than you," Janie teased.

Dee nodded. "They'd have to, wouldn't they?"

JESSE JOINED UP WITH a couple of the bull riders he knew who were looking for a ride into Gardiner. They congratulated him on his win, then spent the rest of the drive dissecting their own efforts, seeking Jesse's opinion on almost every point of their rides.

At the edge of town, he asked where they were headed.

"Well, there's The Bear Claw," Pat Winfrey said. "They've got a dance floor and a country-western band tonight."

Ace Christopher leaned forward from the backseat. "Ruffians has pool tables and a jukebox. I could eat a double order of the chiles rellenos without any help."

"We've got two nights," Jesse said, trying to get into the spirit of the weekend. "We can hit one now, one tomorrow."

They decided on The Bear Claw because the service was faster. "And the girls like to dance," Pat added.

Judging by the crowded parking lot at The Bear Claw, most of the rodeo riders had come up with the same idea. Country music blared through the open door and windows into the cold night air, where groups of smokers stood huddled together, talking, drinking and puffing.

The wait for a table would be a good thirty minutes, Ace was told at the front desk, but they were welcome to hit the bar. A layer of drinkers three bodies deep made a chore out of even asking for a beer.

Finally, Jesse got a deep draw of cold brew. He could have stood in the same place and downed the entire mug, but Pat grabbed him by the elbow.

"Let's check out the dance floor. Most of the unattached girls will be there, waiting for an invitation."

"Sure." He saw that Ace had already started plowing through the crowd between the bar and the dance floor in the other room.

Taking another gulp of beer, hoping that would lift his mood, he followed.

The band on the stage could hardly be seen behind the lines of dancers on the floor and the spectators surrounding them. Being a little taller than the average rodeo rider, he could see over most of the heads in front of him.

And the first thing he saw when he focused on the line dancers was a curvy figure in a bright red shirt and black jeans. She wore her hair braided down her back and bangs cut straight across her dark eyes. Janie.

Jesse wanted to turn around and walk out, but the crowd pressed in and he was stuck standing there, staring. He already knew she was a good dancer. Her rounded hips and bottom accented the words in the song, her cheeks were flushed, her eyes bright. She'd rolled her sleeves up to her elbows to reveal her slender arms and wrists, accented with silver bracelets. Long silver earrings dangled against her neck. He remembered the smooth skin along her throat, and behind her ears....

After what seemed like forever, the song ended with the dancers in their final pose. As she applauded, Janie turned to grin at a calf-roper type who'd been dancing behind her. Next thing Jesse knew, the roper had Janie by the hand and was twirling her around under his arm.

The lead singer for the band stepped up to the microphone. "For a breather, ladies and gents, let's try out a two-step!"

Like pieces of a kaleidoscope, the dancers reorganized into mostly pairs, with some singles still working in lines on the outside. A fast four-beat tune started up and couples began to move. Jesse kept his eyes on the crowd as he eased through a gap that had opened up in front of him.

There they were. Janie and her roper, together again.

He stood there through two more numbers, finishing his beer while watching Janie and the roper dance. Woody was his name, Woody Black. He was a big guy—roping was the only rodeo event where size was an advantage—and fairly handsome, if she liked the dark-haired type.

Maybe Janie did. She'd danced with the same guy three times in a row. Had she come up to Gardiner especially to see him?

Maybe the kisses between them really had been "no big deal."

Ace turned up beside him. "Lot's of choice this weekend. See somebody who looks good?"

"Yeah." Jesse tapped the bottom of his mug against his palm.

"Well, go for it, man." Ace clapped him on the back. "Time's a'wastin'."

"Okay." Jesse handed Ace his mug and stepped through the press of bodies, polite but undeterred. At the edge of the dance floor he paused, catching sight of his quarry again. He snagged lots of other glances, too—blue gazes, greens and hazels, blondes, redheads and brunettes. All of them signaled a willingness to hold his hand and dance.

Instead, he followed Janie to a tall table on the side of the room where she stood with Woody Black, a blonde girl and a bareback rider who already had his hand on the blonde's butt. Jesse knew him, and that was his standard operating procedure.

"Hey, Ted." Stepping up to the foursome, he nodded to the bareback guy. "Saw your ride tonight. Good job."

"Thanks, man. Here's hoping we both win again tomorrow night." Ted picked up his mug and toasted in

Jesse's direction. The blonde beside him was staring at Jesse with round eyes and an open mouth. Next to her, the roper was frowning at him.

Only one person hadn't looked in his direction.

"Hey, Janie." He turned sideways and put his elbow on the table. "I didn't know you'd be here tonight."

"She's with me," Woody Black said before Janie could answer.

Jesse opened his eyes wide. "Really? You brought her here? You paid her cover charge?"

"Well, no—"

"You bought her dinner?"

"Stop it," Janie told him. "He's just being nice."

He held up his hands in surrender. "Okay, no problem. I just wanted to understand the situation, so I'd know if I could ask you to dance."

Finally, her gaze met his. "Why?"

"That's what you do here, right? Find somebody you like and dance with them?"

"Sometimes you dance with a person just to embarrass them."

Jesse saw the fear in her eyes. She didn't trust him. "I'd never deliberately embarrass a lady." He hoped she could hear the promise he was making. Holding out his hand, he smiled at her. "Would you like to dance?"

"Janie—" Black put a hand on her arm. "I asked the band to make the next one a waltz."

"Thanks," Jesse said as Janie placed her fingers in his. Then he walked her to the floor. Her hand came to his shoulder and their palms connected, skin to skin.

He drew a deep breath, feeling Janie shiver as he slipped his arm around her waist. The band started up a George Strait cover, perfect for a close-contact dance.

They moved around for a minute in silence, getting used to the tempo and each other.

Finally, Jesse drew his head back so he could see her face. Janie lifted her chin and gazed at him for several turns.

Her shoulders lifted on a sigh. "Now what?" she asked.

Chapter Nine

"We keep dancing," Jesse said. "It's a waltz."

Janie turned her head to look away, trying to get her feelings or her reactions—something about this situation—under control.

"I didn't chase you up here," she said into his ear. "I didn't know you were riding." The problem with talking was she had to bring her lips close to his face, allowing her to inhale traces of sweat and soap and the scent that was so much a part of him.

He nodded, increasing the torture. "I read your name in the program after I saw you. I should have told you I was coming. You should have told me." When he shrugged, she felt the movement with her whole body. "We could have driven together. Although—"

"Although?" She waited as he led her through two turns.

"That wouldn't make things any easier."

Janie took a deep breath. "No."

The remainder of the song passed in silence, but there was plenty of communicating going on, as Jesse's body spoke to hers. His arm tightened and loosened around her waist and his fingers splayed across her hip, guiding her with small changes in pressure that felt all too much like a caress. His thighs brushed hers or pressed into her as he led in a different direction. Janie stared at the V formed by his unbuttoned shirt collar, mesmerized by the tanned skin and the hint of chest hair, the movement of his Adam's apple as he swallowed.

The song ended, but Jesse's hold on her didn't loosen until the band leader stepped up to the microphone.

"Okay, folks, let's get everybody out on the floor with an easy line dance. Come on, you all know the Electric Slide!"

Lines of dancers started to form around them and Jesse finally dropped his arms. "I guess we should find a place," he said loudly into her ear.

Janie glance toward the table where Dee—and Woody Black—waited. "I should probably go—"

"Oh, no, you don't." Jesse grabbed her hand and dragged her into an empty space. "We're not finished yet."

Three line dances later, Janie begged for a break. "Really, I've got to slow down and catch my breath."

"That last one was fast." Jesse cupped her elbow and steered her toward the back of the room, away from Dee and Woody, who'd glared at them the entire time they'd been dancing. "Let's get a drink."

The noise from the crowd at the bar drowned out any attempt at conversation. Standing next to Jesse as he waited, Janie would have thought she was dreaming except for the press of bodies around her, the smell of cowboys and beer and, most of all, the clasp of Jesse's hand around hers.

Just as he stepped up to the bar, a wave of cold air swept across Janie's back. She turned her head to see people backing away to her right and her left as Woody stalked directly toward her.

"Let's dance," he said, in a tone laced with anger. "Now."

"I'd like a drink first." Janie held up a hand as if she could stop him. "Then I'll be glad—"

Jesse turned around just then, a mug in each hand. He surveyed Woody with a cool blue stare. "You're in the lady's way. Get lost."

Woody clutched at the hand Janie held in the air. "She's coming with me."

Jesse narrowed his eyes. "I don't think so."

Janie could already see where they were headed. "This is ridiculous. I'm thirsty. Let me cure that problem, Woody. Then we'll dance."

The two men just stood there, facing off like bulls in the pasture. Eyes locked, neither of them moved a muscle.

Janie turned to Jesse and pulled the mug of ginger ale from his right hand, sloshing some on his fingers. She took a sip, then another. Two more, then she'd go—

"Well, well." The man's voice, pitched to be heard over all the noise, came from somewhere deep in the crowd. "Looks like The Iceman has finally started to melt."

"You losers better start counting your money," someone else yelled. "If you been betting against The Iceman ever finding a cutie to warm him up, looks like you're gonna be payin' out. He's only human, after all!"

Janie took her last sip and shoved the mug back at Jesse, sloshing yet again. "Okay," she said, turning to Woody. "Let's go dance." She had to separate these two before the situation got out of hand.

"Hey, Woody, weren't you in pretty deep against ol' Iceman, here?" Another anonymous voice.

Woody snarled. "Yeah. And I'm holdin' to my bet. She's comin' with me."

He pulled Janie toward him and she let herself move forward, just to end the confrontation. But she couldn't help a backward glance of apology toward Jesse, left standing with a mug in each hand.

She was almost out of the bar when the first voice sounded again. "Hey, Iceman, now you know what life's like when you're not J. W. Cody's oldest boy. Sucks, don't it?"

The two plastic mugs bounced against the concrete floor. Jesse strode through the splash and sliced into the crowd.

Janie found herself suddenly free as Woody dropped her hand and joined the fight.

Within seconds, most of the men present were throwing punches and taking hits. Most of the women were standing just behind Janie in the wide doorway to the bar, screaming and screeching.

Janie stood with her arms crossed, furious that her night out had to be spoiled by a bar brawl. A bar brawl that Jesse started.

The sound of sirens approaching didn't diminish the violence. Men still wrestled with each other as the sheriff's deputies waded in to separate bodies and write up tickets. Among the last to be hauled outside were Jesse and Woody.

"You're Jesse Cody, right?" A young deputy flipped open his notebook as Janie came up close behind Jesse. "The Iceman?"

"Just Jesse Cody," he said wearily, supplying the address and phone number requested.

"I understand you started the fight?"

"I didn't stop it, anyway." Jesse glanced over at

Woody, answering the same questions a hundred feet away. "I wouldn't say I threw the first punch."

"You had an argument with that guy?" The deputy nodded at the roper. "What were you arguing about?"

"Beer."

"I heard there was a girl involved."

"Nope."

Janie stepped forward. "Don't be an idiot, Jesse." She looked at the deputy. "I'm Janie Hansen. I danced with Woody Black, and then with Jesse. We were getting drinks when Woody tried to make me dance with him. Then somebody in the crowd starting talking about betting on Jesse having a girlfriend."

She'd spoken up without realizing the truth might be embarrassing. Typical. Her cheeks flushed as she went on. "Jesse tried to locate the guy who was harassing him. That's when the fight started. Everybody was primed for it."

While the deputy wrote that down, she braved Jesse's fierce stare to check out the injuries to his face.

"Not too bad. A black eye," she told him. "Bruises and a split lip."

"And a two-hundred-dollar fine." The deputy ripped a page off his pad. "Disorderly conduct."

"No problem," Jesse said quietly.

"Oh, sure," Woody yelled. "Two hundred—hell, two thousand—is no problem for any of them damn Codys. They walk all over the rest of us 'cause they've got the big bucks."

The deputy stepped between Jesse and the roper. "I suggest you get to wherever you're staying, Mr. Cody. I don't want to leave the two of you here to start this whole thing over."

"Not a problem." Jesse gave Janie a sideways look. "Where's your friend? Are you two staying together?"

"Um…" Janie scanned the remaining crowd, looking for Dee. "I don't see her. But I've got my truck. I'm ready to go."

Jesse nodded. "Good." He took a step forward, faltered and hissed a breath through his teeth.

Janie caught his arm. "What's wrong?"

"Nothing major." He took another experimental step and hissed again. "I twisted my knee a little, coming off the bull tonight. And I guess I must have twisted it some more inside."

"Dancing or fighting?"

He shrugged. "I'll be fine."

As they walked toward her truck, however, his limp got worse. He leaned against the fender of the truck as soon as they reached it.

Janie saw pain in the set of his mouth. "Can you even drive?"

"Sure." But his shoulders slumped a little, and his face was pale with fatigue.

"Why don't I give you a lift to where you're staying?"

"Are you going into the taxi business? I'm okay, Janie, really." He stood up straight. "Have a good night. I'm sure I'll see you around the show tomorrow." His first step, with the sound leg, went well.

The second step, onto his bad knee, dropped him to the ground on his butt.

Janie sank to her knees beside him. "Maybe you should see—"

He shook his head. "I don't need a doctor. I'm just tired, maybe punch-drunk." Then he sighed. "But I probably shouldn't drive. If you could…"

"No problem." She helped him to stand up, but left him to get to the passenger side of her truck by himself. Cowboys did have their pride.

Once she had the motor running, she remembered they hadn't arrived together. "Will your truck be okay here overnight?"

"The county sheriff is a friend of ours. I'll call and ask him to get it moved to the hotel sometime tonight."

Janie gazed at him. "The sheriff is your friend? Why didn't you tell the deputy? He would have forgotten about giving you a ticket."

"I deserved a ticket as much as anybody. And, as your friend pointed out, two hundred dollars isn't much for me."

She stayed quiet for a minute, pondering how she'd agonized over buying a hundred-dollar coat for Las Vegas. "So, where are you staying?"

"The Lodgepole Inn."

"Oh. Me, too."

He stared straight ahead. "Then you won't have to go far to get to your room."

That was looking on the bright side if ever she'd heard it.

Turning into the parking lot of the Lodgepole Inn a short time later, she saw the usual rodeo hijinks in process—cowboys and girls standing around in open doorways with cups and bottles in their hands, lots of laughter and teasing going on.

Jesse stirred beside her. "My room's on the other side. If you wouldn't mind dropping me off, I'll keep my limp to myself."

"No problem." Janie had spotted Dee in the door of the room they shared, with her arms around the waist of Woody Black's hazer. They'd obviously paired off, for the evening at least. And the last thing Janie wanted to do was stand around and watch them getting cozy.

On the other side of the motel, things were much quieter. Doors were closed, lights off. "I'm about halfway down," Jesse directed.

Once she'd parked the truck, they sat in silence for a minute. Finally, Jesse sat up straight.

"Thanks for the ride, Janie." He put a hand over hers, still resting on the steering wheel. "And even more for the dances. I had fun."

She dared to meet his eyes. "Me, too." Seeing how his eye had swollen shut, she had to ask, "Would you like some help? I could make up some ice packs, bandage cuts."

He hesitated so long, she knew she'd been stupid to suggest such a thing. "Never mind—"

"Actually, I'd appreciate the help." He smiled at her. "Especially the ice."

"Oh." Janie couldn't restrain her own smile. "Good."

Too many trips to the hotel ice machine would raise questions, so Janie drove to a nearby convenience store for ice and drinks. In the meantime, Jesse called the sheriff, then wrestled off his boots and jeans. The stiff denim had made a pretty good brace, keeping the swelling to a minimum, but by the time he rolled up the leg of the sweatpants he'd donned for sleeping, his knee had evolved into a football-size mess, stained purple and blue and red from well above his knee all the way down to the top of his clean sock. With every minute, the pain escalated.

He was sitting on the end of the bed, his foot braced on the only chair in the room, when he heard the key turn in the lock. Carrying bags in each hand, Janie jerked to a stop in the open doorway.

"Yuck," she said matter-of-factly, after her first glance at his leg. "Are you sure it's not broken?"

"Pretty sure." Wincing, he bent the knee to put his foot on the floor, and had to grip the bed on either side of him to keep from passing out. "Just needs ice and a handful of pills," he said, when he could talk. "I'll be fine."

"Here's the ice." She took the ten-pound bag into the bathroom and brought back cubes in the hotel ice bucket. "I got plastic bags, too." She set a shopping sack on the table. "Pain pills, in case you didn't bring any. Drinks." Two plastic bottles of soda appeared. "Plus food. I don't know about you," she said, with a shy glance in his direction, "but I didn't get any real dinner. The pizza smelled too good to resist."

"A woman after my own heart." He took the ice-filled plastic bag she handed him and placed it on his knee. The ache intensified. "I didn't count on starting a bar fight before I ate."

She turned from the table and looked him over. "Wouldn't you be more comfortable with that leg on the bed? Here—" Before he could answer, she began folding the covers back and arranging the two pillows against the headboard.

Straightening up, she stepped back from the bed. "Now you can be comfortable. Or maybe you want a shower? Although I can't imagine standing on that leg on wet tile would be too safe. You could take a bath—"

Jesse put up a hand, laughing. "Whoa, lady. Why don't we eat, first? Pour out some of that soda and pull me off a couple of slices."

Janie nodded decisively. "Good plan."

They were so hungry, they both finished off their first slice without talking. Jesse glanced over as he reached for his third piece and saw that Janie had put her second one down.

"You okay?" he asked.

"Sure. I was just—" She hesitated. "Just thinking."

He sat back against the pillows, waiting. When she didn't speak, he prodded. "About?"

"The fight. They called you Iceman."

"Yeah. Stupid."

She looked at him, he dark eyes troubled. "I'd heard your nickname on the circuit. Even your brothers call you Iceman sometimes. I'm just wondering…why?"

Keep it simple. "I don't show much emotion when I'm riding. I don't let on that I'm nervous or excited. I guess folks see that as 'ice' in my veins. Iceman."

Janie nodded, but didn't look convinced. "I wondered if it had something to do with Laurie."

Now Jesse put his pizza down. "She's been gone a long time."

"But you loved her very much. You were getting married."

He blew out a sigh. "Yes." They'd been only weeks away from the wedding when cancer took her life.

"You still wear white hats, like she asked you to do."

"In this business, you want people to remember you. There aren't too many white hats in the rodeo arena."

"And you don't…you haven't…had a steady girlfriend since. They call you Iceman because your heart is frozen. No woman has warmed you up."

Until now. "I've been working hard, at home and on the circuit. There hasn't been time for—for a relationship."

The warmth in Janie's face cooled as he watched. She straightened in the chair and picked up her pizza slice. "That's what you told me in Vegas," she said. "Better be careful, Jesse. If you wait till there's enough time, you might find yourself turning into an Iceman for real."

They finished the rest of the pizza without conversation. Jesse swallowed the last bite of the last piece and sighed. "I might just live, after all." He leaned forward to get a soda bottle off the table, putting all his weight on his bad knee. With a groan, he threw himself backward on the bed. "Or maybe not."

When he opened his one good eye, Janie stood over him. "C'mon, Jesse, get into the bed. You know you need to keep your foot up, ice your knee and get whatever sleep you can."

The thoughts that streamed through his mind had nothing to do with ice and a lot to do with the body heat generated by just looking at Janie Hansen.

Which meant that lying flat on his back right in front of her, wearing soft sweatpants, was not a good idea.

"Right." He curled to sit up again, bringing on a whole host of aches in his chest and belly and back. He'd have been better off if he'd blown his ride on the bull—he would hurt less. And chances were good nobody would have wanted to take him down a notch at the bar.

But then he wouldn't have stolen his dances with Janie. He'd rather break a leg than give up those minutes holding her in his arms.

Standing up and limping sideways to the head of the bed took all his willpower. He sank thankfully onto the mattress again, used both his hands to lift his hurt leg and even let Janie pull the sheet and blanket up to his waist.

"That's fine," he said, before she could starting tucking him in. "If you'll hand me the pills and a glass of soda, your official duties will be over for the night."

He'd set his personal pain-relief arsenal on the dresser next to the TV. Janie went to pick up the bottles but then—nosy woman that she was—stopped to read the labels.

"This is heavy stuff." She held up one of the narcotic prescriptions. "If you take too much, you might not wake up."

"I'm careful." He held out his hand for the meds. "I know what works best for whatever happens." Selecting one pain-relief pill, he swallowed it with a gulp of soda. "See? That's it for tonight. All I need is to be able to sleep. And I'm tired enough, that one dose should put me under."

She gazed at him, her brows drawn straight and low over her eyes. "If you say so, I'll leave the extra soda by the bed in case you're thirsty." Then she wrote her name and 259 on the notepad by the lamp. "That's my room. If you need something, call." Once more, she favored him with a shy, sweet smile. "Even if you just want somebody to yell at because you can't sleep."

Jesse nodded. "Will do. Now get to your own room. You're riding tomorrow, too. I'm planning to be there to see you win."

Her face brightened and flushed at the same time. "That would be terrific. If you were there, I mean." She backed toward the door. "And if I won."

"Like tonight," he reminded her.

"Oh, that's right. I did win, didn't I?"

"Uh, yeah. Good night, Janie."

"'Night, Jesse. Keep your leg up."

She closed the door and, to his relief, did not return.

Jesse wasn't sure how much longer he could have pretended he wasn't near screaming with pain. Pain and frustration.

His knee cap might very well be broken. He remembered coming down hard on the concrete floor at the bar, with another guy flung across his shoulders as added weight.

Making a decision, Jesse reached for the high-powered prescription bottle and poured out a dose. He needed to sleep, and mere pain relief wouldn't help.

To get any kind of rest, he'd have to forget the shape of Janie's curves under his hands, the press of her breasts against his chest. She'd spoken into his ear, and the whisper of her breath on his skin had driven shivers down his spine and all the way into his fingertips and toes. He'd seen her lips up close, knew how plump and luscious they would feel under his. Maybe, if he fell asleep quickly, he wouldn't have to remember those impressions—until the morning, anyway.

And if he slept heavily, deeply enough, he wouldn't have to think about how much differently this night might have ended.

JANIE LEFT HER TRUCK where she'd parked it, near Jesse's room, and walked around to the other side of the Lodgepole Inn. The partying continued on an even wilder note than when she'd first arrived that night. Sleep would be almost impossible with all this noise going on.

When she reached the room she shared with Dee on the second floor, she discovered the door closed and the curtains in the window drawn. Most distressing was the do-not-disturb sign hanging on the doorknob. What did that mean?

As Janie stood staring, Marina Dodge, the woman she'd beat earlier to win her race, sauntered by. "They won't poke their heads out till late tomorrow morning, if then."

"They?"

"Dee and the hazer for that guy who dumped you. Don't remember his name. Anyway, they got it on hot and heavy out here, then went inside and closed the door." She grinned maliciously. "Better luck tomorrow night."

Janie leaned back against the deck rail and tried to think. Dee had a man in their room. Asking him to leave would cause an argument, and she didn't want to sleep in that bed now, anyway. She hated spending the night in her truck—she always woke up with her back stiff and her legs cramping. The cold would make everything worse. And it had just become very important to win tomorrow's race.

No other option seemed to be available. But settling into the backseat proved a futile effort—though she was short, the seat was shorter. She didn't have a pillow or a blanket. The driver's seat wouldn't recline far enough, so she couldn't stretch out flat. What a miserable night this had become.

Turning onto her left side, she felt something stick into her thigh…something in the pocket of her jeans. Grumbling, she twisted around, arched up…and pulled out the key to Jesse's room.

His room would be dark and quiet. Warm. She could sleep in the chair, with her head on the table. Or… or…

Not giving herself time to think, she slipped out of

the truck and left it locked behind her. The empty sidewalk and closed doors were her only witnesses as she tiptoed to Jesse's room, slipped the key gently into the lock and turned the knob.

She pushed, and the door opened. Releasing the breath she'd been holding, she stuck her head into the room. "Jesse? Jesse, are you still awake?" She'd only left about ten minutes ago.

He didn't answer. Janie set one foot inside, then the other. "Jesse? Jesse, can you hear me?"

A mumble came from the head of the bed.

She went to stand over him. He lay with his injured leg on top of the covers, the bag of ice still on his knee. Otherwise, he didn't seem to have moved since she left.

"Jesse, can you hear me?"

His good eye opened. "Janie?"

"It's me. I can't get into my room."

"Bad." At least, that's what she thought he said.

"Could I sleep here tonight?"

"Sure…" The word tapered off into a soft snore.

Janie straightened up. Okay, she'd asked, he'd answered. She'd be staying in Jesse's room tonight. Pulling the chair to face the table, she sat down and rested her head on her folded arms.

A few minutes later, she stretched her legs out in front of her, slouched down and leaned her head back against the edge of the vinyl-covered back cushion.

Next, she tried leaning her head to the right, on her shoulder. Then to the left. She rested her chin on her chest. She curled up on the seat and tried to lay her head on the arm.

An hour passed before she finally admitted that she could not sleep in the chair. A second's consideration told her she would not sleep on the floor of a hotel room except in case of out-and-out disaster. Same with the bathtub.

Which left only the bed.

Chapter Ten

Jesse kept his eyes shut and let consciousness seep slowly into his brain. As soon as he moved a muscle, every part of his body would start to hurt—might as well put off the agony as long as possible.

He'd rested well, anyway, considering the state of his knee and all the other bruises he'd collected last night. Somehow, he'd managed to roll onto his left side, where he usually slept best. He was warm and comfortable and the room smelled like flowers. What more could he ask?

Then he thought, *Flowers?*

Jesse took a deep breath, pondering that scent. He cracked open his good eye…and pretty much stopped breathing altogether.

His left arm stretched across the bed beside him, as usual. Janie was sleeping with her head on his upper arm, which was absolutely not the usual. That explained the perfume.

Though startled and confused, Jesse didn't move or make a sound. No normal man would complain about the position in which he now found himself—sharing his bed with a sexy woman. Janie lay curled up facing him. Her hair brushed his chin, and her hand rested lightly against his chest.

He could have stayed this way forever. Or at least for the rest of the morning.

But Janie stirred, then smiled. Jesse couldn't help smiling, too. What a great way to greet the new day.

Then she froze. And gasped. Eyes closed, she whispered, "Jesse?"

"Yep."

"I meant to be gone long before you woke up." Her hands came up to cover her face. "I am so embarrassed."

The long black braid of her hair lay across her shoulder. Jesse reached over with his free hand to finger the shiny strands. "Nothing to be embarrassed about. But how did you get here?"

She peeked out between her fingers. "You don't remember?" When he shook his head, she groaned and hid her face again. "Now I'm totally humiliated."

When she started to roll away, Jesse put a hand on her elbow, keeping her still. "I don't understand."

"You probably think I crawled in beside you on my own," Janie wailed. "Just for fun. Or—or expecting something."

"Those aren't such bad options."

"But I asked first. I did, really." She lowered her hands. "When I went upstairs, Dee had a guy in the room with her. I tried to sleep in my truck, but then I thought maybe you wouldn't mind…I didn't mean to bother you."

"You didn't." *Unfortunately,* his mind added.

"I did ask, and I thought you heard me."

"I might have. I don't remember. Those pills…"

He let his voice fade, suddenly less interested in an

explanation for last night than in exploring the possibilities of this morning. Janie lay beside him, soft and warm and heavy-eyed, with her scent in his head and her plump lips only inches away. Her breasts rose and fell, brushing against his wrist as he held on to her elbow. A cowboy could only resist so much temptation.

"I'll just get out of your way," Janie said, again trying to move away from him.

"Well, you know," Jesse drawled, "there is the matter of rent in this situation."

"Rent?" She gazed at him for a moment, then must have read his intentions in his face. Laughter flickered in her eyes. "Really? How much rent?"

"One or two. Maybe three."

"Dollars?"

"Nope." He lowered his mouth toward hers.

"Ah."

The first kiss was well worth waiting for. Janie's lips, soft and slightly parted, welcomed his advance. They yielded slightly to the pressure of his mouth and then, with a small sigh, responded with a gentle demand of their own.

Needing a breath, Jesse lifted his head. "One."

"Not enough?" Janie asked, pretending to pout.

"Not nearly."

A more experimental kiss, this second one, and more breathless, as well. With a hand on Janie's shoulder blade, Jesse drew her closer, until they lay pressed together from chest to knee. She slipped her arms around his shoulders and her hand under the neck of his T-shirt, then stroked her palm across his back in all directions, as far as she could reach.

Jesse groaned at the pleasure of her touch. "Two," he muttered. And took them straight into number three.

After only a few minutes, he'd forgotten what they were counting, or why. Need rose inside him, fierce and hot, burning away the threads of his control. Under his clumsy fingers, the buttons on her red shirt slipped free, allowing him access to the creamy skin he'd spent so much time thinking about. Janie got rid of his T-shirt completely, then used her mouth and hands on his chest to destroy the last of his sanity. Much more of this craziness, and he wouldn't remember his own name.

With her hair draped across the tips of his fingers, he rubbed his knuckles along the line of her jaw. "I want you, Janie. After all these years we've known each other, I saw you in Las Vegas and it hit me right between the eyes. Now I can't seem to stay away from you."

Her dark eyes caught a stray beam from the light through the window. "But you said—"

Jesse shook his head. "I know. I thought I could shut this off, somehow. But I'm not having much success. Are you?"

"I've never been able to shut off what I feel for you." When he would have pulled her closer, she resisted and rolled away. "What about all those obstacles between us? Mark, your parents…"

He took a deep breath in his turn. "None of that's changed, has it?"

"Not that I can tell."

"Mark will hate us being together."

She nodded.

"My dad will be furious."

"My mother would be, too, if she understood."

"But—" Jesse took her shoulders in his hands, turning Janie to face him. "But I don't care. Whatever anybody else thinks or says, this is about what we want. Isn't it?"

Her palms came to rest on his chest. "Yes."

He grinned and drew her body toward his. "So…"

"Your knee—"

Jesse swore. "Janie?"

"Yes?"

"Shut up and kiss me."

And still she tried to argue with him. "Why don't you kiss me?"

Holding her gaze, he nodded. "Not a problem."

He didn't take it slow or make it easy on either of them. His first kiss ravaged her mouth, his lips and teeth and tongue demanding a fiery response. Sweeping over her face, he absorbed the smoothness of her cheeks, the slope of her nose and the point of her chin, then moved on to the intricate spiral of her ear and the fragrant angle between her shoulder and neck. Janie tossed her head from side to side as he touched and tasted, until that black hair of hers was a silky web, binding them together in desire.

Only minutes later, the remainder of their clothes had disappeared and they lay twined together, inventing caresses to drive the passion between them harder, faster, hotter. Janie dragged her hands along the backs of Jesse's thighs and buttocks, then raked her nails over the same path.

"Vixen," he growled, and she grinned.

"Devil," she panted, when he drove her to the edge of control, only to back off at the last second.

Soon enough, though, she was begging and he was beyond desperate. Murmuring, "A cowboy always brings his own equipment," Jesse moved away for a moment, then returned to her arms. "Let's dance, Janie girl. You and me."

She had no words, Janie decided, for the experience of having Jesse's body joined with hers. Ecstasy seemed too easy. Completion couldn't be big enough. With the thrust of his hips, her entire universe exploded...and then realigned, settling into a blinding, breathtaking pattern she would need the rest of her life to understand.

Or maybe, she thought—as he began to move and she went to him, with him—maybe the word really is that simple, after all.

Happiness.

JESSE WOKE UP BECAUSE HIS knee throbbed and his head ached. Otherwise, he might have believed he'd died on that bull last night and gone to heaven, because he'd never felt so good in his life.

Janie's head rested on his shoulder, her bare leg curled around his knee, and her hand lay on his chest. Every morning should start out exaç tly like this.

Then the phone rang. The first bad news was having to pull away from Janie to reach the receiver.

And then he said, "Hello?"

"Got a news report that you'd been put in jail last night. What's going on?"

"Good morning, Dad."

"Your mother's worried sick. Are you okay?"

"Sure." He'd explain the knee when he got home.

"Did you win?"

Jesse could hear his mother's protest in the background. He grinned. "Yes, sir, I won."

"That's better. Listen, come straight to the house when you get home Sunday. We're having everybody for dinner, and then I've got something to say to the whole family. See you there."

Without anything as formal as "goodbye," J.W. ended the call.

Jesse hung up the phone and turned back to Janie. "Where were we?"

She moved easily into his arms, but her face was troubled. "Have we made a mistake?"

He brushed her hair back from her face and shoulder. "I have no complaints."

"They will."

"We'll deal with that when we can't avoid it." He kissed his way along the arch of her collarbone. "We don't have to let them spoil this morning, do we?"

Janie's sigh of pleasure was all the answer he needed.

AT THE END OF SATURDAY NIGHT'S competition, Janie and Jesse stood together in the arena accepting gold belt buckles for their individual championships in barrel racing and bull riding. Along with all the other winners, they waved and smiled as the crowd applauded.

Then they retreated to his room for their own private celebration.

Sunday morning, after eating breakfast together under the interested gazes of most of the rodeo participants, they got ready for the long drive home.

Saying goodbye turned out to be harder than Jesse expected. Janie and he were heading to the same place, more or less. He'd see her tomorrow, when she came to work on Sundae's leg. For that matter, he could see her every night of the week if he asked her out.

But letting her drive off without him didn't feel right, even though he'd be driving right behind her. Behind the horse trailer, anyway.

"Be careful," he said stupidly, when he'd run out of anything else he wanted her friend Dee to overhear.

"Bye," the blonde called, wiggling her fingers from the passenger side.

"Good to meet you," he told her, then realized he'd already said that once, after the two women had climbed into the truck.

Janie gave him a smile that seemed too bright for the occasion. "Bye, Jesse. Have a good drive. If you feel tired, or your knee hurts, take a break..."

"I'll be fine." He slapped the roof of the truck cab and stepped back, refusing to say anything else for fear he'd get himself in trouble.

He didn't catch up with Janie because he didn't try. Shadows lengthened as he traveled and the white-coated mountains loomed from the right as he drove toward the Shoshone River valley and the Cottonwood Ranch. Passing through Markton, he glanced along the road leading to the Hansen property and thought about stopping, but didn't lift his foot off the gas pedal. Life was complicated enough—there was no sense in starting up rumors at home, too.

Passing through the ranch gate, Jesse heaved a huge sigh of relief. He could heat up some stew for dinner, take a few pills and zone out with a ball game on TV.

Then he remembered. Before he could zone out, he had to check in with the parents. That meant bypassing the old homestead he lived in by himself now and driving another three miles to the new house.

What did his dad plan to say? Was this the payout on whatever J.W. had been planning in Vegas? Jesse chuckled, remembering Janie's suspicions of a Cody family plot. Would those nefarious motives finally be revealed this evening?

He parked at the end of a long line of family vehicles—including Mark's truck—and limped along the stone driveway, then climbed three different angles of steps to reach the massive front door. The house consisted mostly of windows, allowing views of the mountains and the river valley from every room. His mother seemed happy there, but he couldn't be sure. She didn't encourage personal questions these days.

Taking a deep breath, Jesse pressed the doorbell button. Inside, a set of chimes played the tune for "Home on the Range." The kids had all thought the choice goofy, but his dad liked it.

When the door opened, Jesse faced his sister across the threshold. "Good to see you," she cried, throwing her arms around his neck. "Your face looks awful. I hope the other guy looks worse."

Before he could say anything or get his arms around her waist to hug back, Elly pulled away. Looking puzzled, she ran her fingertips lightly across his right shoulder, back and forth. "That's an interesting aftershave you're wearing," she said, and leaned in again to sniff at his collar. "Smells like roses, maybe some gardenia and lavender."

Then her lower jaw dropped and her eyes went round as she stared at him. "I know that scent," she whispered. "I gave it to her." She cast a glance over her shoulder, toward the living room. "Jesse Cody, why do you smell like my best friend?"

"Close the damn door," J.W. shouted. "It's cold as hell in here already."

Jesse did as ordered. "Janie competed at the Gardiner rodeo," he told Elly, walking past her. "And that's where I've been." Without giving her a chance to ask any other questions, he joined the rest of his family around the big stone fireplace in the living room.

J.W. had set the stage for this family get-together. A huge blue spruce tree sat in front of the largest window, decorated with his mother's favorite ornaments—different sizes of green glass balls, pine cones frosted with silver glitter and garlands of green and silver ribbon. Underneath the tree ran a toy train set, currently being observed with rapt attention by Matt and Clay. Dex and Josie sat close by, keeping an eye on the youngsters.

To complete the scene, J.W. occupied his big armchair beside the fire, with Anne perched on a low stool at his knee and the rest of the family arranged on nearby sofas and the floor.

Jesse actually looked over his shoulder, wondering if there was a photographer setting up to take pictures. And wondering exactly what the rest of them were being set up for.

"Come sit down," J.W. ordered. "We're not eating till I get this taken care of. That end of the couch is empty."

Jesse followed his nod and saw that his dad wanted him on one end of the couch with Mark on the other and Nicki in between them.

"Thanks," he said, and went to the wide hearth on the opposite side of the fireplace from J.W. He'd rather choose his own seat, even if that meant sitting on stone.

J.W. narrowed his eyes but didn't comment. "I called you all here," he said, "because I've got a couple of things to tell you. There are gonna be some changes at the Cottonwood Ranch in the new year."

Jesse crossed his arms over his chest. *Here it comes.*

The Cody patriarch cleared his throat. "Just before the National Finals, I had some medical tests. This week, the doctors told me I've got prostate cancer."

Sitting up straight again, Jesse let his arms fall to his sides. Absolute silence held for nearly a minute.

Then Elly said, "Oh, Daddy." With a sob, she buried her face against Will Jackson's chest.

"This is not the end of the world," J.W. continued, but he had his hand firmly on his wife's shoulder. "I have every expectation of being here to give you all grief for decades, yet. But in order to save my energy for the fight at hand, I will be playing a less active role in the ranch management.

"Nothing is settled as of yet. I'll be talking to each of you, getting a feel for how things are best settled. That includes Mark and Nicki because they are part of the family now."

J.W.'s steel-hard gaze honed in on Jesse with that statement. Jesse called on his best poker face to greet the challenge. This wasn't a time for arguing or giving in.

"I thought it was fair to warn you all about what's coming—what I'll be doing after Christmas and why I'll be calling on each of you. Also, I'll be rewriting my will to reflect the changes taking place. And…"

He looked around, then stared into his wife's face for a moment. "And that's all. Let's go eat."

While the rest of them sat paralyzed, J. W. Cody left his chair, helped his wife to stand and then escorted her, with his familiar, slightly limping gait, across the entry hall and into the dining room.

As soon as he could move, Jesse followed his parents. But instead of joining them at the table, he stalked across the marble floor as fast as his injured knee would allow, jerked the door open and slammed it behind him as he left the house.

THE KNOCK ON THE DOOR came at 9:00 p.m. Sunday night, just as Janie sat down to dinner. She put her head in her hand for a moment—the drive from Montana had been a long one and settling her mother for the night had taken the last two hours. Now she sat alone to eat, cold and hungry and sad.

When the rap repeated, she pushed back from the table and stood up. "Okay, okay," she called. "Since when do you knock to come in, Mark? This is still—" She opened the door.

Jesse stood outside, shoulders hunched against the wind-driven rain. "Hi. I probably should have called but, to be honest, I didn't want to give you a chance to say no."

Janie found her voice. "I wouldn't say no. You're welcome."

He stepped past her into the house, his body big and solid and *here*. She felt warmer just having him in the room.

Standing in the center of the living room, still wearing his coat, Jesse lifted his chin and sniffed. "Smells good." He looked toward the kitchen. "You were eating. I'm sorry."

"It's not a problem." She hesitated a second and then said, "Have you had supper?"

His blue eyes met hers with a bashful expression. "Uh…no."

"Why not? Wait…" She'd just remembered where he was supposed to be tonight. "What about the family meeting and dinner? Your dad—"

The look on Jesse's face prepared her for something bad.

"Take off your coat and come sit down," she told him. "You can have some leftover chili with me."

Once they were both served and seated, Jesse told her between bites what his father had said. "I didn't get any specifics. I don't know what kind of treatment he's having or what his plans are for the ranch. I just… couldn't stay."

"I am so sorry." She put her hand over his left one, resting on the table.

"I've been driving around, thinking, going nowhere. All at once, I realized I'd come here." He sighed and squeezed his eyes shut, then rubbed them with his fingertips.

Janie cleared her throat. "We always seem to think our parents will be with us forever."

"Yeah." He started to say something else, but a noise from the back of the house interrupted.

"Janie? Janie?" The weak voice was her mother's. "Janie, where are you? Something's wrong, Janie."

"I'm sorry," Janie said.

Jesse shook his head. "Don't worry about it."

"Janie?"

"It's okay, Mom. I'm coming."

But her mother already stood at the opening from the hallway into the kitchen, clinging to the edge of the wall. Her unbuttoned nightgown drooped off of one shoulder, her feet were bare, and her eyes were wide and scared. At least her hair looked neat, because Janie had washed and braided it before putting her to bed.

She went over and circled an arm around Abby's shoulders. "What are you doing out here without your

robe and slippers? You'll catch cold. Let's go back to
your room—"

Abby's terrified gaze was fixed on Jesse. "Who is
that man? Why is he here?"

He stepped forward. "I'm Jesse Cody, Mrs. Hansen.
Elly's brother."

"You remember Elly, Mom." Janie used a hand on
her mother's cheek to turn her head so their eyes could
meet. "Elly is my best friend."

Abby turned to stare at Jesse again. "Cody," she said,
moving her mouth as if tasting the word. "John Walker
Cody."

Jesse said quietly, "I'm his son."

"I remember." She nodded, but then her eyes narrowed and her mouth thinned. "John Walker Cody. Lied
to me. Never said he was married…how was I to know?
I showed him, though. Didn't want help. Didn't want
him—or her, the bitch—interfering with my son."

Janie couldn't bear to see the pity and disgust in
Jesse's face, couldn't think of what to say. Without a
word, she turned her mother back toward the bedroom,
holding her close, keeping Abby's head on her shoulder
with her free hand. Jesse would, she assumed, let himself out.

An hour later, she left her mother sound asleep again,
stretched out in the center of the bed rather than cower-
ing next to the wall. For herself, Janie only wanted a
glass of water and a full night's rest. Maybe by morning
she'd be able to think about tonight's disaster without
getting sick to her stomach.

As she came down the hallway, she could see into the
living room beyond the kitchen. There sat Jesse Cody
on the end of the sofa, an elbow propped on the arm to
hold up his head. While she watched, his hand dropped.

He lurched to the side, startled, then braced his head again and relaxed. The man had fallen asleep waiting for her.

After he'd cleaned up the kitchen.

"Jesse." She sat down beside him on the couch and gave his sound knee a shake. "Jesse, wake up."

His thick blond lashes slowly lifted. "Hey." He yawned. "Sorry. I fell asleep."

"What are you doing here? You should be at home in bed."

He shook his head, waking a little further. "I didn't want the night to end…like that. Is your mother all right?"

"No worse, anyway." Janie stared down at her hand, still resting on his knee. "I apologize for what she said. When she was well, she didn't think those things. I never heard her say a word against your parents. Ever."

Jesse's hand came to rest on hers. "It's good to hear the truth, for a change. And maybe she's just let J.W. off the hook a little. Sounds like she didn't want him to know Mark at all."

Fear shot through Janie's chest. After ignoring Mark for thirty years, J. W. Cody was trying to make amends. What Abigail had or hadn't wanted, all those years ago, wouldn't change the present situation.

And an old letter from Abby to J.W., written that fateful year but returned to its sender still sealed, shouldn't matter, either. Certainly not to Jesse, or any of the other Cody kids. Mark had read it, but he'd discovered his parentage by comparing blood types and appearances. He'd only found the letter afterward—a confirmation, of sorts.

So Janie didn't have to feel guilty for not telling Jesse about a letter no one cared about, anyway—even if she'd been the one to find it in the first place, and had kept the secret to herself for more than two years. Who cared?

While she debated, Jesse reached around her for the coat he'd left on the sofa, then stood to shrug into it. "I'd better go. We both need some rest. This dilemma has waited thirty years—it'll wait another night, at least."

Janie followed him to the door. "It's always been a complicated situation."

His face softened. "But we can't do anything about any of it tonight, can we?" Bending, he brushed her mouth with his.

"Not a thing," Janie whispered.

"Sleep tight," he said with a last, sweet kiss. "See you tomorrow at the barn."

And then he limped out the door to drive home in the sleet and get into his cold bed alone, just as Janie got into hers. She could only hope Jesse slept better than she did.

But she doubted he would. He had so much on his mind tonight—his dad's illness, of course, and all the problems arising from it. Mr. Cody had included Mark in the "family" meeting, and though he hadn't said anything specific, she could tell that the gesture had rubbed Jesse's already raw feelings. How would he reconcile his worry over his dad with his honest dismay at the man's behavior? Bad enough that he'd been unfaithful to his wife, but then to ignore his own son…

For Jesse, honor and responsibility went hand in hand. His dad's choices, even if they didn't affect Jesse directly, would complicate their relationship.

Punching her pillow, turning over and over again as she tried to find a restful position, Janie thought about the letter she'd found and concealed. Though not very important in itself, the returned note still seemed like a time bomb, ticking away quietly until it exploded at the worst possible moment.

And she had the feeling that her own chance to be happy with Jesse—her opportunity to make him happy—might be blown to dust at the same instant.

Chapter Eleven

Anne went to bed late in the evening, after the children had eaten dinner, asked all the questions they could think of about John Walker's illness and his future, then left for their own homes. But she hadn't been able to sleep.

Now she sat at her kitchen table, the mug of tea she'd brewed hours ago gone cold between her hands. As the rising sun streaked the sky with red and gold, the palisade of tree trunks along Cottonwood Creek in the backyard gradually became visible. Unlike the sun, however, Anne was so deep in thought she hadn't moved for a long time.

So deep, in fact, that she didn't hear J.W. come into the kitchen until he put his hand on her shoulder.

"So this is where you're hiding."

"Aack!" She jumped, and the tea spilled. "You scared me."

He chuckled. "Well, what are you doing sitting here, just staring out the window?"

"Thinking." She scooted her chair out with an irritated jerk. "For heaven's sake, hand me a dishcloth to mop this up."

He gave her a startled glance as he reached for the towel. "What are you so upset about?"

Blotting the table, she didn't answer at first. "Jesse," she said, walking into the kitchen.

Her husband waved a dismissive hand. "He's always the quiet one. He just didn't feel like talking about what's going on."

Wringing the towel into the sink, she shook her head. "It's more than that. There's enough unsettledness about the situation involving Mark without—"

Her husband made a chopping motion with his hand. "I don't want to argue about Mark anymore."

"I don't want to argue, either. In fact, I'm trying very hard to cooperate with you as far as he's concerned. But—"

"Look, Annie." He came close and reached for her hand, cradling it between his palms. "I've done what you asked. All these years, I never made a move toward Mark. He seems to believe his mother would have kept the secret to her grave, if she hadn't gotten sick. But now he knows—"

"Along with everybody else in Wyoming."

"—and I owe him the dignity of acknowledging him as my son."

"What else does he think you owe him?"

John Walker shook his head. "I don't know yet. We're still trying to get acquainted. Can't you give us the time we need? It's not easy catching up on thirty-one years."

She looked down at their joined hands. "I'm simply asking you to remember that you have five children who are no less precious simply because you've known them all their lives. Especially Jesse."

"What I remember is that I love you." His arm curved

around her waist and drew her to him as he bent to kiss her. Despite her anger and disappointment, Anne surrendered to her husband's passion. For more than thirty years, she'd been cherished by this strong, lustful man. He had given her children, a home and every luxury she could imagine. He shared with her the power and influence of the Cody name.

Her life could be very much worse. Many men in John Walker's world took women for granted, used them like toys and expected their wives to accept a promiscuous lifestyle they would not change. John Walker had strayed only once in their marriage. He'd spent the years since trying to make amends in every possible way. Abby Hansen's son was the only reminder of that awful time.

The only reminder…except for Anne's own, endless guilt.

WHEN THE BELL ON THE FEED store door jangled at nine on Monday morning, Janie looked up from the cash register to see Elly Cody coming along the aisle toward her.

"Don't you look Christmassy," she said, admiring her friend's fuzzy white scarf, red sweater and dark green jeans tucked into black boots. "All you need is a red cap with a white ball on the end. We've got some dog hats like that over in the corner."

"If only." Elly gave her a hug, harder and longer than their usual greeting. "I'm more in the market for a miracle."

Janie drew back and took in her friend's red-rimmed eyes and pale face. "Is this about your dad? I'm sorry, El. I know you must be worried sick."

Elly pulled a tissue out of her pocket to dab at her

eyes and nose. "I can't believe he just dropped it on us out of the blue. Right before Christmas. Nobody had any idea that he was sick."

"Well, that's the problem with prostate cancer, right?" The store was empty except for the two of them, so she led Elly to sit down on a nearby horse mounting block. Then she turned over a big bucket nearby for herself. "You don't know unless a doctor checks. But they have all sorts of effective treatments available these days. Lots of men have recovered completely."

"Oh, believe me, Will and I stayed up half the night reading every article on the internet. It's just…I don't want to lose my dad." With a sob, Elly folded her arms on her knees and buried her face in them.

Janie rubbed her friend's back and made soothing noises, thinking about Jesse's reaction last night to the same news. And she couldn't blame either of them. She knew from experience the fear and heartbreak this kind of announcement brought. Even though she hadn't been as close to her dad as Elly was to J.W., she'd mourned the loss of a parent. Two parents, really. Her mother's decline was happening in phases, rather than all at once. But in the end, she would be gone.

"And Jesse just walked out." Elly jerked herself up again. "He didn't say a single word—not 'I'm sorry' or 'What can I do' or anything. Sometimes he makes me so mad."

Moving back, Janie spoke carefully. "He's just as upset as you are, El. But Jesse's not one to lay his feelings out for everybody to see. You know that."

"We all needed him to be there, to help us sort this thing out. Instead…" Elly sat motionless for a moment. Her blue-green gaze focused on Janie's face. "You already knew about Dad before I got here. You knew what his illness was before I told you."

Janie gave a slight shrug.

"Jesse left Mom and Dad's house…and went to yours?"

"Yes." She swallowed the huge lump in her throat. "He did."

"Why?"

She wasn't quite sure herself. "I guess he needed somebody to talk to."

Elly stood up. "Jesse doesn't discuss Cody business with anyone outside the family."

Janie got to her feet. Temper jumped into her throat. "That would change, I expect, if he found a woman he cared about."

Her best friend stared at her in shock. "You and Jesse? Is it serious?"

"Um…maybe." For her, at least.

Elly brushed her blond hair back with both hands. "I can't believe…I mean, you had a crush on him back in school, but I figured you'd given up when he and Laurie got engaged. And she's been dead for eight years."

Janie suddenly saw a shelf that needed straightening. She went to work. "We got better acquainted in—in Las Vegas." Thank goodness no one else was in the store. "And we both rode in the Gardiner rodeo this last weekend."

"He mentioned that last night. And I knew you two took in some of the sights in Vegas. Then something happened, and he acted like a bear with a thorn in his paw for ten days. You spent the rest of the time hiding in your cave. Did you have some kind of argument?" She shook her head. "That would explain a lot of the crazy behavior."

"We didn't exactly argue." But her flushed cheeks probably betrayed the truth. "So, anyway, last night, when he needed somebody to listen, he came to my house. I'm sorry if that bothers you."

"Bothers me?" Elly swooped down on her and wrapped her in another frenzied hug. "I think it's great. My best friend and my big brother—you're perfect for each other." She glanced around and then lowered her voice as she looked at Janie again. "Have you slept together?"

Stunned at the sudden about-face, Janie could only nod.

"Oh, excellent. The Iceman has melted. I'm thrilled, really." She bestowed a kiss on each of Janie's cheeks. "Has he proposed?"

"No!" Janie backed away. "And if you say a single word to him about that, or to anyone on the planet about what I've told you, I will never speak to you again, Ellen Anne Cody. I swear. Jesse would hate having anybody know."

Elly wrinkled her forehead. "Well, aside from the fact that, as I said, he doesn't like talking to people about Cody business, why would he hate having people know that you're going together?"

"We aren't. Really. It's all just…happened."

"Pooh. You've loved him for decades."

"He doesn't know that. And I don't know that he feels the same way." Tears sprung to her eyes as she took her friend by the shoulders. "Please, please, Elly. I'm so afraid the least problem will drive him off. Just let us work this out in our own time."

"Well, sure. Okay." They walked together back to the checkout desk. "I get to be your bridesmaid, right?"

At that moment, the doorbell rang. "If I have one, you're it."

"Good." Elly blew out a deep breath. "At least this gives me something else to think about. Thanks."

"Think about it by yourself. No sharing." Elly opened her mouth but Janie intercepted the question. "Not even Will."

"Okay," she whined. "I'll see you at the barn sometime later this week. I've got a great idea for your Christmas present."

Janie grinned. "Can't wait."

But as soon as Elly had left, the grin died. Janie could only hope her friend would keep the promise and keep quiet. The news that she and Jesse were…together…was bad enough. Coupled with J.W.'s recognition of Mark as his son, the situation would provide endless fuel for gossip and speculation. Jesse was already sensitive to the talk about him and Mark.

And the more people who talked, the greater the possibility that he would find out the last piece of the puzzle—Abigail's letter—from someone else. Janie couldn't imagine how anyone besides herself and Mark, and J.W., of course, would know. But the risk was real.

So she would have to tell him soon. At the right time, in private, where he could be furious if he wanted.

Where he could kick her out of his life with no one else the wiser.

MONDAY NIGHT, JESSE MADE a point of remaining at the barn so he could see Janie when she came to treat Sundae. He was already in the stall, giving the horse a carrot to munch on, when he heard her quick footsteps coming down the hallway.

She gave a little jump when she saw him. "Oh, hi. I didn't realize you were here."

"Yeah, there's no way to warn somebody, is there?" As she turned to make sure the stall door was latched, he came up behind her and slipped his arms around her waist. "I guess I owe you an apology for yelling at you last week."

"You're forgiven." She drew a deep breath as he kissed the side of her neck, and shivered as he lifted her braid to brush his mouth over the little mole hiding underneath. "You're also wicked. I'm here to take care of your horse."

"He's used to waiting on me."

Janie leaned her head back to look at him, and he took complete advantage, covering her lips with his. Her generosity amazed him—she gave whatever he asked, then offered more, twisting in his hold to press up against him and tighten her arms around his back. Jesse could have laid her down on the floor and taken her right there in the stall. He damn sure wanted to. Needed to.

But he still had a shred of sanity left in his brain. "Sundae's bored," he whispered, trying to catch his breath.

"I'm sure." She retreated an unsteady step, holding on to his waist for balance. "He deserves some attention."

With a deep breath, she bent to pick up the bag she'd let fall and crossed to the horse. "I know," she murmured, stroking his neck. "You're the handsome one. But he pays the bills, so I have to make him feel special."

Chuckling, Jesse sat down on the floor with his back against the wall. "How was your day?"

She shrugged, beginning to stroke Sundae's injured

leg. "So-so. Elly stopped by—she's really upset about your dad."

"Yeah. I had a phone call today from Walker. Also Dusty and Dex and Elly. Each of them yelled at me for leaving last night. And then they each gave me their version of the situation and what we could do." He let his chin sink to his chest. "I told them Dad's a competent adult. He'll make his own decisions on this, and all we can do is support him. None of us, not even Mom, is in control."

"It's natural for them to look to you. You're the oldest."

"I should have left a message giving them Mark's number. He's the oldest." He didn't avoid the glance Janie sent his way. "I'm not being mean. There's just nothing else I can say."

She nodded and resumed her work. They talked off and on during the process, about how her genetics final had gone last week and when the rodeo season would start up again in January. Jesse watched her massage Sundae's back, shoulders and neck, and his own body started to ache.

"I could use a good massage," he said as she began to pack up her supplies. "What do you think?"

She smiled as she came across the stall. "I think your idea of a massage is not the same as Sundae's."

They stepped out into the aisle, he made sure the stall door fastened and then turned to set his hands on her shoulders. "I don't know about that. Sundae stayed a stallion for six years. He probably has lots of good memories."

Her palms cupped his elbows. "Memories are all he has these days, I guess." She lifted her face, and her lips parted in a sweet, sexy smile.

"Poor guy." He took a kiss. And another. "Making memories is so much better than just—"

"Remembering them?" Janie laughed up at him.

"Exactly." Slipping his palms down her back, he drew her close. "Like this."

Las Vegas. Montana. And now at home. Where he kissed Janie Hansen didn't seem to matter—each encounter consumed more of him. Each kiss burned hotter, and his desire flared higher. At this rate, he wasn't sure he'd last a lifetime before burning up.

But what a way to go.

When he lifted his head the next time, they were leaning against the wall. Her shirt was unbuttoned, the front clip on her lacy black bra unfastened. His shirttail hung outside his pants. And he was crazy with need.

"My house is empty," he said as she dragged her mouth across the hollow behind his jaw. "Let me take you. There." Her tongue touched his skin. "Please."

Janie kissed his jaw, his chin, his temple and his mouth. But then, with a sigh, she pulled back. "I have to go home." Her hands shook as she tried to put her clothes back where they belonged. "Alma won't stay all night. So I…can't stay here."

Frustration slammed into his gut. He'd felt this tightness in his belly once before, after being kicked by a two-ton bull. Yet he knew he couldn't argue. Janie was right to put her mother first. This was just sex. Right?

Like hell, came the answer.

It didn't change what had to happen. Janie would be going home and he would take a cold shower.

The reason, though, made a whole lot of sense. This was what you did for the woman you loved.

"Okay." He tried to help her with her buttons but their fingers tangled together, so he stepped back and kept her coat folded over his arm until she was ready for it. They held hands on the walk to her truck, and Jesse managed to keep their goodbye kisses out of the incendiary zone. Barely.

"See you tomorrow early," he told her, brushing the hair he'd loosened behind her shoulder. "Drive safe."

"You, too." She smiled at him, touching his cheek. "'Night, Jesse."

"Sleep tight."

He watched the taillights of her old truck disappear into the darkness before getting into his own vehicle for the three-mile sprint to the coldest shower in town.

ALL THE STRESS, THE LATE nights and missed sleep finally caught up with Jesse. He didn't wake up until almost ten on Tuesday, missing Janie's visit to the barn and almost missing breakfast, as well. A glance out the kitchen window showed him a heavy gray sky just now beginning to spit a mix of ice pellets and flakes. Six to eight inches were forecast for today and tonight, followed by colder temperatures that would keep snow on the ground through the holiday. A white Christmas was on its way.

The Cottonwood Ranch gave its workers as much time off as possible during the holidays. The cowboys took short shifts, with a skeleton crew going out morning and evening to spread hay for the cattle. The Codys, themselves, looked after their own horses, along with the animals in the barns and the paddocks nearby. Everybody tried to relax, to take their time and just enjoy the season's pleasures—Mom's cooking, the decorations and the carols and the chance to be together. Family was the essence of a Cody Christmas.

This one might be different, given the family's

changed circumstances. Jesse wasn't sure exactly how they were supposed to celebrate when J.W. had developed this serious illness. Sure, men came down with prostate cancer all the time, got treated and appeared cured.

But some of them died. And Jesse wasn't ready for that. As aggravating as his father could be, as furious and confused as Jesse felt over the Mark Hansen issue, he wanted his dad around to argue about it.

Of course, typical of J.W., he'd turned the situation to his advantage, deciding to reorganize the family business and rewrite his will at a point where no one would want to upset him because "Dad is sick." This was probably the plot Janie had sensed in Las Vegas—J.W. getting his own way. Mark Hansen might not have spent much time with the rest of the family, but he'd have to be a cold man to argue with a cancer patient.

Moving slower than usual, Jesse got to the barns around noon and took care of the lunchtime feedings— grazing animals did best with small amounts of food throughout the day rather than huge meals spaced twelve hours apart, though they could adjust if they had to. Elly had made up a chore schedule and posted it on the barn bulletin board, and he checked off Tuesday midday as a signal that the task had been taken care of. Stalled animals didn't get much exercise, so their rations had to be downsized accordingly. Seconds at lunch were not allowed.

His footsteps echoed on the concrete floors as he walked through the stallion barn, today occupied only by the horses and him. He enjoyed the peace of the buildings without people in them. Humans always had a purpose, an agenda, to keep them hurrying forward. Animals, on the other hand, simply lived the day.

As he came into the cattle barn, however, Jesse heard

two male voices...or else one man talking to himself. The tones seemed almost identical. He followed the sound, softening his footsteps, until he located the conversation in the big conference room near the ranch office.

The door stood slightly ajar, and he could identify the speakers now—J.W. and Mark. Maybe J.W. had chosen this time when nobody was around to conduct the threatened—er, promised—interview having to do with rewriting his will.

Jesse did not intend to eavesdrop. But just as he turned toward his office and the exit door, their voices raised and words became distinct.

"Look, J.W., I appreciate what you're offering." Mark Hansen sounded frustrated. "I'm just not sure that it's what Nicki and I want for our life."

"How could you not want a part of all this?"

Jaw clenched, Jesse could picture his dad's gesture—widespread arms embracing the Cottonwood Ranch and the whole Cody empire.

J.W. continued his sales pitch. "I'm not proposing to make you rich, son."

Jesse fisted his hands at his sides.

"But you'll need a homestead, and this little property I've got my eye on would be perfect. I'll give it to you and Nicki as a wedding gift, throw a prize Cody bull or two and some cows in for Christmas. What happens then is up to you."

"That's really generous, J.W. But—"

"I've got this bull breeding program, son, and nobody to supervise while I'm getting through this cancer thing. You could do that for me."

Mark was silent for a minute. "I think it's too much, too soon."

"What the hell does that mean?" J.W. didn't like being told no.

"Three months ago, I had no idea you were my father. I—"

"That's bull. I think you've known for years you didn't belong to that drunkard."

"You're wrong." A chair scraped across the floor. "And I'll thank you to be respectful." Another pause. "Anyway, I just want time to become comfortable with you and the rest of the family. Then I can think about how involved I want to be with your business."

"Your business, too. I'll be dividing my interests among you kids in my will. Wouldn't you like to work with me, get a feel for things before you have to run the show by yourself?"

"I hope that'll be a long, long time from now."

"Maybe. Maybe not. It would be good to have you working as a Cody as soon as possible. And—I know this is a tough one—I'd really like you to consider taking my name."

"What?" Mark's voice echoed Jesse's shock.

"Makes sense. You're a Cody—why not make it legal and official?"

After a pause, Mark said, "No."

"Think about it, son. The advantages—"

"No." Louder. Footsteps approached the door, then stopped. "You know, you've got a lot of gall, suggesting something like that. You must think the Cody name is right up there with God Almighty."

"Now who's being disrespectful?"

"Thirty-one years, dammit! For thirty-one years you ignored my very existence. I didn't get a look from you if we passed on the sidewalk. All those junior rodeos—

you showed up with your 'real' sons, but did I ever get so much as a nod when I beat their pants off?"

"I had my reasons. I could never be sure you were my son."

"You might have asked. Or you could have opened the letter she wrote."

Without thinking further, Jesse stepped through the conference room door. "What did you just say?"

Both men jerked around to stare at him.

"That's right." Mark propped his hands on his hips. "Janie found a note in Mom's papers a couple of years ago. She wrote to your dad, wanting to talk to him about the situation. But he couldn't even be bothered to read the damn thing. He sent it back unopened."

Jesse stared at his dad. "What kind of man are you?"

J.W. levered himself out of his chair and came to stand between Mark and Jesse. "I don't know what the hell you're talking about. I never saw a letter."

Mark snorted. "Yeah, right. That's about the only excuse for your behavior. Too bad—"

Gripping Mark's elbow with a still-powerful hand, J.W. turned him so they stood face-to-face. "I swear to God, and on this land I love as I love my own life. I never saw a letter from your mother."

Feeling a hollow under his ribs like he'd just been sucker punched, Jesse dropped into the nearest chair. He braced his elbows on his knees and pressed the heels of his hands against his eyes.

"Then who?" He asked the question with his face still hidden. "Who tried to prevent J.W. from knowing about his *other* son?"

Chapter Twelve

The front door slammed with the thundering crack of a nearby lightning strike.

Coatless and hatless, Jesse stormed across the entry hall and down the hallway to the doorway of Anne's office. She got to her feet as he halted on the threshold, shoulders heaving with the force of his breath.

"Tell me." His mellow voice emerged in a growl. "Tell me you didn't do this."

Anne supported herself with her hands flat on the desktop. "Do what?" Hope flickered feebly in her heart.

"There was…a letter. From Abby Hansen."

The last spark winked out. "Yes."

"You sent it back without letting Dad see it?"

She drew a deep breath. "Yes."

Her son's face contorted with pain. "Dammit, Mother. Why?" He dropped his head back and stared at the ceiling. "How could you be so cruel? You, of all people?"

"Jesse." She left the shelter of her desk and crossed the room to put her hand on his arm. "Please, son, try to understand."

But Jesse jerked away from her touch. He walked to the window wall overlooking the backyard and Cottonwood Creek, where snow now fell thick and fast. "I will never understand how you could separate a man and his son."

"I didn't know she was pregnant when I sent the letter back. I didn't read it."

"You would have noticed, soon enough. I thought family meant everything to you."

"It does!" She came to stand behind him, but folded her arms around herself. "My family, Jesse, is more important to me than my own life. That's why I had to... had to—"

"Shut the bastard out? For God's sake, Mother, he was a baby. A little boy." Jesse covered his face with his hands. "He looks just like Dad."

"But what would have happened, Jesse, if your father had tried to do right by two families? Two women?" She moved around to his side. "I was so afraid of losing him. Who could say that John Walker wouldn't choose to be with her? She was pregnant, and I wasn't. I'd lost my baby. Would I ever have another one?"

Jesse wiped one shirtsleeve across his eyes, then the other.

Anne cleared her throat. "If her child was the only Cody baby, I might have lost my husband. I loved him so much, Jesse. I couldn't bear the thought. And then, when I did get pregnant...all I could think about was protecting that baby. Protecting you. Making sure that your father was present every single day to love you and teach you and give you what you deserved as his son."

"And so you sentenced that other kid to life with an abusive alcoholic who never provided a decent standard of living for his wife and kids. Am I supposed to thank you?"

"If you could just realize—"

"Oh, I realize. I realize that my entire life has been perfect, at the expense of another human being whose only fault was being conceived without a marriage license. That all the years I've fought and struggled to make Dad proud were just wasted effort."

"Jesse, no!"

"Oh, yes. I never stood a chance of actually being good enough on my own, because who and what I am, as an individual, never really mattered. All that counts is the label. I'm the lucky one born with the name Cody and so I get the prizes—the money, the gifts, the job and the land and—and—"

He wheeled away, but not before a graveled sound, half laugh and half sob, escaped.

Anne let her own tears fall unheeded.

Jesse came to rest in front of a bookcase, where photographs of the kids going back as far as first grade shared the shelves with trophies and handmade gifts. He fingered different objects, moving from one to the next with a shaking hand. Finally, he picked up a small plate, decorated beneath the glaze with two bright red handprints. The words *World's Best Mom* and *Love, Jesse Cody* painted in shaky cursive letters, arched around the edge.

"I remember making this," he said. "Fourth grade. You were the brightest, best person in my world."

She extended a hand, pleading. If he destroyed the plate, she didn't think she could bear it.

Her son, her blue-eyed cherub, flashed a cold glance in her direction. "No, I'm not going to break it. I'm not much into symbolic gestures." Carefully, he set the plate back on its stand. "I'm going to let you keep that reminder of everything you meant to me. Then."

His shoulders lifted on a breath, and the tension flowed out of his body. "I'm not even going to stamp out in a rage and swear never to darken this doorway again. The family's got some hard times approaching, with Dad being sick. These days will be tough on you, since you love him so much."

Anne winced as she heard the edge of sarcasm in his words.

"Just know what you've done to that little boy." He tilted his head toward the plate. "I've been mad at Dad since I discovered who Mark's father had to be. But I never thought J. W. Cody was perfect. He's always walked a fine line between hero and outlaw. That's just who he is.

"No, I saved my illusions for you. I looked at you and I knew what being good meant. I wanted to follow your example."

Shaking his head, Jesse returned to the door. "I guess it's just another demonstration of my Cody luck—I made it all the way to the ripe old age of thirty before my illusions got shattered." He shut the front door quietly as he left.

RUTH AND LESLIE PEARSOLL had wanted to go into Cody for a Christmas concert, so Janie told them she would close the store and lock up for the night. She never felt nervous being alone—Markton wasn't the kind of place serial killers liked to hang out. Strangers stuck out like a sore thumb. And she counted all the citizens as her friends. No one would think to hurt her.

Still, she had to admit to a little jump of nerves when

she stepped out the back door of the store into the heavy snow and saw a truck parked next to hers. In the next second, she recognized the Cottonwood Ranch sign on the door panel. Jesse was here.

Unfortunately, the thought didn't soothe her anxiety. Distracted by his kisses, she'd failed in her plan to tell him about the letter last night, and the barn had been empty except for the animals this morning.

Was now the time?

She swallowed hard, crossed the powder-coated parking lot to the truck's passenger side and opened the door. "Hey, cowboy. Looking for some company?"

"Sure," he said. But he didn't smile. "Climb in."

He'd left the engine and the heater on, so she settled herself in the seat and unbuttoned her coat. "I didn't expect to see you until later, at the barn. What's going on?"

With his right wrist propped on the steering wheel, Jesse stared at the snow piling up on the windshield. "We had a little drama today out at the ranch."

"Is everybody okay? Is Sundae all right?"

"Sundae's fine."

"Who isn't?" She waited through a long silence.

"There was a letter."

The words struck like hammer on anvil. Janie closed her eyes.

"Your mother wrote a letter to my dad about the baby she was carrying. Turns out, he never even saw it."

"What?" She opened her eyes to stare at him. "How do you know?"

He gave a harsh chuckle. "The envelope wasn't open when you found it. Still sealed. Is that right?"

"Yes."

"My mother got to the letter first." Without seeing

him, she would never have identified this hard voice with the man she loved. "She sent it back without showing him, or opening it."

"Oh, Jesse." Janie slumped back against the seat. "I'm sorry."

He nodded. "I'm…surprised. I would have never expected her to be so selfish."

"There were reasons, I'm sure—"

He held up a hand, stopping her. "Excuses, maybe. But what legitimate reason could there be for denying a child his father? This wasn't the nineteenth century. Even thirty years ago, people could be rational about these situations."

Janie waited through a long silence, willing to listen, hoping that being heard would soothe some of his pain.

With a sudden move, he pounded his fist against the steering wheel. "All my life, I looked up to her…to both of them. He showed me what strength and courage could accomplish, the value of hard work and a quick brain. She…"

His voice choked off. He shook his head and cleared his throat. "She taught me honesty and respect, for other people and for yourself. And all the time, all my life…" He stared straight ahead. "She lied."

Janie put her hand on his arm. "Jesse—"

He moved away from her touch. "I trusted her," he said after a pause, in a disbelieving voice. "I grew up with a healthy skepticism concerning J.W.—by the time I was twenty, I knew he could be a sneaky SOB. But she was never less than perfect. How could I have been so blind?"

Janie closed her empty fingers. "You're in shock. Give yourself time to adjust." She'd been afraid of just this reaction. A man with such high ideals couldn't let go easily. "You've had a hard couple of months, Jesse. This will all make more sense when you've had time to think."

"Maybe." He shrugged one shoulder. "Or maybe I'll go on without ever understanding. There's always work needing to be done. If I'm lucky, I'll just get numb."

The bleak prospect chilled her. "The holidays are coming. You'll be able to talk to your parents, work this out. I'll do whatever I can—"

He started shaking his head. "Talk changes nothing. They made their decision—they chose to ignore the fact that Abigail was pregnant, that she gave birth to a son who looked just like J.W."

Suddenly, he chuckled. "Mark was there, though. Every junior rodeo I entered, his name was on the list. He beat me, more often than not. And J.W. stood by, watching Mark Hansen take home the trophies, all the while knowing *his son* was the winner—the son he'd refused to claim. There is some justice, after all."

Letting his head fall back, he didn't say anything else for a long time. Janie waited, longing to touch him, wishing she could somehow make things better.

Knowing she was, in her own way, part of the problem.

Finally, he straightened up and blew out a breath. "You should be getting home. It's dinnertime."

"Come with me. I'll make a meatloaf and mashed potatoes…"

Jesse was shaking his head. "Thanks. But I think I'll head back to the ranch."

The resignation in his voice scared her. "What are you thinking? About…about us?"

He sighed. "What I said in Vegas was the truth, Janie. Now is not a good time for me. I—"

"You're wrong, Jesse. You should have someone of your own now, more than ever." It didn't matter that he was a rich Cody and she was just poor Janie Hansen. She loved him, and he needed that love. "Don't shut me out."

"I need some time," he continued, as if she hadn't spoken. "Like you said. And some space, to figure things out."

"You can figure things out with me."

But Jesse shook his head. "You've got your own life to lead—vet school just around the corner—and your mom to take care of. The last thing you should have to deal with is my family's troubles piled on top of your own."

"That's it? The end?" Could she make him angry? Would that help?

For the first time in a long time, he looked directly at her. "I'm sorry. I can't ask a woman to share my life until I figure out who the hell I am."

Her heart ached for him, but she ignored the urge to soften. "In other words, slam, bam, thank you, ma'am. I guess the rodeo guys were right—The Iceman can't be melted. Silly me, for thinking I was different."

Emotion flickered in his eyes, but he didn't react with passion. "Take care, Janie. I'll be thinking about you."

She may not have made Jesse mad, but she'd worked herself up into a temper. "Go to hell," she told him as she opened the door beside her.

"Already there, sweetheart." Jesse laughed as she dropped down into the snow. "I'm already there."

Janie put her whole weight into slamming the truck door as her only reply.

JESSE WAS SITTING AT HIS DESK in the old homestead when Elly slammed the front door behind her and came in.

"Hello, sister," he said, lifting his half-empty beer in a toast. "What brings you out in the blizzard?"

"You." She jerked off her scarf, hat and gloves, then shrugged out of her coat and dropped the whole pile on the leather couch. "What are you trying to do, Jesse?"

"Finish this beer so I can drink another one. What are you trying to do?"

"Keep this family from self-destructing."

"You're about thirty years too late, girl."

She came around to where he sat with his feet up on the desk. "Come on, Jesse. You don't have to be so bitter."

"What have I done? I got to the bottom of the story, and now I'm at home by myself, not bothering a soul."

"You left Mom on the verge of a breakdown. And Janie called me to say you could take care of your own damn horse. I guess that means you broke up with her."

He took another drink. "There was nothing to break."

"So you're just going to pretend nothing happened between the two of you?"

"Pretty much."

"She's loved you most of her life, you know."

With the bottle halfway to his mouth, Jesse paused to look at his sister. "No, I don't."

Elly shrugged one shoulder. "She had a crush on you in junior high. And high school. As far back as I remember, you're the only guy Janie ever talked about."

"That's absurd. I was engaged to be married, and that was a long time ago."

"I didn't say she was smart about it."

He sat and thought about the years, forgetting the beer. "I don't believe it."

"Well, you don't have to believe me. Ask Janie. On the other hand, Mom—"

Jesse dropped his feet to the floor and stood up unsteadily. "No. I'm not talking about it." He headed for the kitchen.

And was followed by his pesky little sister. "Can't you see her side?"

"No." Grabbing a beer from the refrigerator, he looked around in vain for a bottle opener. "Where'd you put it?"

Elly shook her head. "Did you consider that she might not have been quite…well, mentally stable at that point? She'd suffered a miscarriage and a long episode of depression."

"Self-defense by reason of insanity? I'm not sure that's a legal option. Give me the opener, Ellen."

She slapped the tool into his open palm.

"Ow."

"You're a self-righteous jerk, Jesse Cody. You haven't exactly been the soul of generosity yourself, as far as Mark Hansen is concerned."

"We don't get along."

"Because you're jealous of his talent. Always have been."

Jesse set his teeth and glared at his sister. "Get out."

"Don't order me around. I've got as much right to be here as you do."

"Fine. I'll get out." Keeping hold of the bottle and opener, he went to the hall closet and grabbed his coat, then headed for the front door.

"Jesse." Elly came after him again. "Where are you going now?"

"Someplace peaceful." Pulling his truck keys from his pocket, he stepped out onto the porch. The snow was still falling, and they had close to a foot on the ground already. "Drive safe," he called back over his shoulder. "See you Christmas Eve."

Climbing into the truck, he started the engine. "Maybe."

THE CALLS STARTED COMING in as early as 5:00 a.m. Fortunately, Jesse had slept on the couch in the barn lounge, so he was there to answer the phone.

"Hey, boss, I've got five-foot drifts out here. If you can handle the hay without me…"

"Boss, my truck engine's frozen. I'll try to get there for the dinner shift…"

And then a call stranger than the others. "Jesse?"

He scrubbed his face with one hand. "Yeah."

"It's Mark. I…uh…figured with all this snow, your cowboys might have a hard time getting there. You need help with the feeding?"

"Could be. Is it still snowing?"

"You bet."

Jesse fell back flat on the sofa. "Great. I'll probably try to move out about daylight, if you can get here by then."

"I will."

With the dial tone still buzzing in his ear, Jesse wondered why, of all his siblings, the one to call and offer help was the least connected of them all. Maybe the rest of them took for granted that the work would get done? It could be that the Cody kids were all just a little bit spoiled. Even him.

But the Hansens never had a chance to be spoiled. Abby had probably loved them for all she was worth, but she didn't have much besides love to give them. Janie worked hard for everything she got. Her brother, too. Jesse had always hated admitting the fact.

Mark arrived at the cattle barn as Jesse sat in the hay truck, warming up the engine. When he climbed into the passenger seat, he handed Jesse a tall travel mug, warm to the touch.

"Nicki made coffee." They both slurped the hot brew for a few minutes.

"I appreciate it," Jesse said as the caffeine began to take hold. "I forgot to turn the pot on before I fell asleep."

"No problem. You ready?"

"Pretty much. I guess we'd better get this done."

Not so long ago, hay for herds of cattle would have been fed in small square bales, thrown out of the back of trucks by freezing cowboys. Modern improvements on the system included a lift for huge round bales, allowing the hay to be transported to pastures and unrolled in a strip on the ground for the cattle to eat. A couple of honks on the horn would bring a herd running.

A crew of just two men still required a fair number of trips to get hay to all of the Cottonwood cattle and horses. Jesse and Mark reached the last pasture shortly before noon. The snow had stopped for the time being, and they sat on the truck bed in the cold for a few minutes, gathering the energy to drive back to the barn.

"Hear that?" Mark asked, cocking his head.

When the wind died down, Jesse thought he heard a cow bawling. "Where's it coming from?"

Mark shook his head. "I can't tell."

"We won't hear her inside the truck."

"Nope."

"That means searching on horseback."

"Yep."

They both swore and hopped down to get inside and drive back for horses.

"Nicki packed up some lunch, too." Mark retrieved a couple of grocery sacks from his truck when they got back to the barn. "I don't know about you, but my belt buckle's bumping against my spine at this point."

"I always knew she was a smart girl…er, woman." Jesse took one of the bags and, out of habit, led Mark toward his office. Realizing, he stopped at the doorway. "We can go to the lounge—"

"Nah. This is fine." Once Jesse claimed the desk chair, Mark sat down across from him. "I just have to get some food in my belly."

They wolfed down the roast beef sandwiches in silence, devouring potato chips and Christmas cookies and shiny red apples with few comments. Once the bags were empty, Jesse sat back with a groan.

"That feels so good. I don't remember the last time I ate a meal." He didn't want to remember.

"Yeah, I expect I'll have a hard time keeping my weight down for the bulls with Nicki feeding me."

"You're gonna keep riding?"

Mark shrugged. "It's fun. I might not push as hard as I did this year. How many times do I need to lose the Finals?"

"Good point." Jesse yawned and stretched. "Much as I'd like to take a nap, I guess we'd better go back out and make sure that cow's not in trouble."

"Right behind you."

Jesse fetched two of the best cow ponies in from the pasture, showed Mark where to find saddle and bridle, and set about getting his own mount ready. The gray gelding he'd chosen, Ghost, knew the work and could be depended on to stand when necessary. But he wasn't Sundae.

"Wish I was saddling up my best worker." He slipped Ghost's bit into the horse's mouth.

"Yeah, it's a shame he's injured. Janie really likes that pinto. Sundae, right? And I've got Beaut, here?" He pointed to the horse he'd just saddled, a dark gold palomino with a silver-blond mane. "As in Beautiful?"

Jesse nodded. Maybe if he didn't talk for a few minutes, the mention of Janie would just slide by without further discussion.

No such luck. "You're wrong to hold her responsible for this mess," Mark said quietly. "Nothing would be different if she'd told you about the letter two weeks ago. Or four."

Jaw locked, Jesse led Ghost toward the outside door.

Mark and Beaut followed. "Janie's pretty torn up," he said, when they both were in the saddle.

"There's a lot of that going around."

In a sudden move, Mark swung Beaut around to block Ghost's progress. The horses stood nose to flank while the two men glared at each other.

"I promised her I wasn't going to hit you," Mark said through clenched teeth. "But you're making that a hard promise to keep."

"I don't want to talk about your sister." Jesse turned Ghost's head, but Beaut moved at the same time—another block.

"So you can just listen. Janie's as honest as they come. She did not deliberately hold that letter back, any more than I did. You need to come down off your high horse and give us all a break, Cody. You're no better than anybody else, maybe not so good as some. Deal."

Then he turned Beaut's head away and went jogging over the snow, following the tire tracks from the truck's earlier return.

Jesse seethed for a couple of minutes, then urged Ghost into the same gait. They had a job to do, and sitting around arguing in the cold would not get it done.

Riding around in a pasture until dark didn't get it done, either. They found the cow soon enough, standing by herself in the corner under a tree, bawling. Jesse got a rope around her head and held her in place while Mark took a closer look.

"Early calf. She's got milk," he said. "Think it died?"

"Probably. Damn, I hate that." Jesse sighed. "And I hate thinking about a newborn calf freezing to death at Christmas. Let's tie her here and see if we can find a carcass."

The snow started up again just as the light began to fail. Now they were searching in the snow-filtered twilight for a calf no bigger than a herding dog. A dog would have been useful, but Jesse's Buddy had died of old age last spring and he hadn't yet had the heart to find a new one.

He snorted at his own whiny attitude. *Poor, poor pitiful me.*

Full dark came down, with snowflakes as heavy as insects landing on their faces. Jesse had lost the feeling in his fingers and feet and his butt hours ago. Giving up had never been part of his vocabulary, but maybe this was the first time. He just didn't have the heart to keep trying.

He and Mark had separated, riding in opposite directions along the perimeter fence, in case the calf had gotten snagged in the wire. At first, Jesse didn't believe the cry he heard in the wind could be real, and he rode on along the fence, squinting against the heavy wet flakes.

Then the call came again, closer. "Mark?" he shouted, standing up in the stirrups.

"Northwest," he heard. Or thought he did.

Blinded and freezing, he let Ghost have his head as they loped toward the farthest corner of the pasture. He saw Beaut at the last minute as he stood braced against the wind, with Mark beside him, down on his haunches in the snow.

"The calf?" Jesse dropped out of the saddle and promptly fell to his knees.

Mark threw him a grin. "Happened to me, too. Yeah. This little guy found a gully to huddle in. I guess his mama wandered off and then couldn't find him under the snow."

"Still alive?" Jesse could hardly speak for the pins and needles in his feet.

"Yeah. But he's got to get warm fast. I'll carry him. You hand him up."

The calf barely protested being picked up by a human and lifted onto the front of Beaut's saddle. Jesse, on the other hand, swore the snow blue as he pulled himself back onto Ghost with his painful hands and feet.

"Let's get the cow," he groaned. "And get out of the cold."

Mama didn't like being pulled along by a rope, especially not in the wake of a horse, and she bleated continuously during the endless ride back to the barn. Speed wasn't really an option, so they ambled, slowly, and Jesse nearly fell asleep with the swaying of the saddle.

They'd probably gone less than five miles from the

barn in their search, but five miles on horseback in day-light didn't take nearly as long as five miles in the dark, on tired horses in deep snow, with a cow in tow. Jesse actually began to wonder if they would make it. The calf had to be dead by now, though Mark hadn't said anything. Men had frozen to death closer to home than this, out in the elements.

Which would be a shame, he thought. Not to see Janie again, or get the chance to apologize for his stupid accusations. She deserved to hear him acknowledge the truth.

So he sat up straighter. He was struggling to keep his eyes open when an unexpected aurora of light on the horizon caught his attention. "What the hell is that?"

Mark didn't appear too alert himself. "Mirage?"

"Don't think so."

"Santa Claus?"

"A day early."

"It's a long trip around the world. He's getting a head start."

They both chuckled, then fell silent again.

At last, when Jesse was beginning to think they would all just lie down in the snow and get some shut-eye, Ghost stopped walking.

"Good idea," he muttered. "We can rest for a few minutes."

"Nope." Beside him, Mark stirred. "Look."

Ahead of them stood a gate. Beyond the gate, not more than a hundred yards off, were the barns. Every outside light, every floodlight and most of the interior lights had been switched on.

And beside the barns was a herd of pickup trucks, headlights blazing and horns blaring. Jesse thought he heard music, too—rock and roll, country or carols. Maybe all three.

"What in the world are they doing?" Mark asked as people standing on the trucks started waving their arms and jumping up and down.

Jesse grinned and dismounted to open the gate. "Welcoming us home."

Chapter Thirteen

"There they are!"

"Where?"

"I see them!"

The entire Cody family had gathered at the barn, once Nicki called J.W. and Anne to tell them Jesse and Mark hadn't shown up by sundown. Now they all cheered and shouted as the horses carrying the two men shuffled through knee-deep snow to get home.

Janie hung back, not wanting to impose but not able to stay away, either. Jesse wouldn't be glad to see her, but she'd needed to know he was safe. Mark, too, of course. She told herself she'd leave in just a minute or two. Really, she would.

The horses stopped just within the circle of light from the barns and trucks. Dusty Cody went to Jesse's horse and Elly took the palomino. Walker stood ready to handle the calf Mark had been carrying—Janie could see the poor thing struggle feebly during the transfer. The mama cow could, as well, and began crying for her baby. Anne had already untied the rope Jesse had fixed to his saddle horn and she led the cow as Walker headed with quick strides into the cattle barn. Dex followed on his crutches. Maryanne waited just inside the barn door with Josie and Paula and their sons, who watched all the unusual activity with wide eyes.

Nicki had rushed to Mark's side and stood beside him as he dropped out of the saddle. He groaned and staggered as his feet took his weight.

"Cold," he said, teeth chattering. "I'm colder now than I've been all day."

"Lean on me," Nicki told him, bringing his arm around her shoulder. Elly led the palomino toward the horse barn. "We've got hot drinks and food inside. You'll be fine."

Mark grinned and kissed the top of her head. "I'm already fine."

J.W. had gone to stand by Jesse's horse. "Coming down?"

Jesse took a deep breath. "I'm thinking about it." He lifted his head as Janie watched, and his gaze met hers across the distance between them. "You go on in, Dad. I can make it."

"Sure?"

"Yeah."

The Cody patriarch nodded and headed into the cattle barn. The big double doors slid closed, blocking out the blowing snow and cold air.

Moving in what looked like slow motion, Jesse stirred in the saddle. Slipping his feet from the stirrups, he leaned forward to swing his right leg over. He hung there for a moment, then slid to the ground…and fell backward flat out in the snow.

"Jesse?" Dusty stepped toward his brother. "Jesse?"

Janie arrived in the next second, dropping to her knees beside him. He lay with his eyes closed. Snowflakes had frozen onto his eyelashes. "Jesse? Say something. Please."

"I'm sorry," he mumbled.

Dusty cleared his throat and looked at Janie. "Can you handle this?"

"I think so."

He gave her a nod and led the gray horse, his head hanging with exhaustion, off to a well-deserved rub-down and dinner.

When Janie looked back to Jesse, he'd opened his eyes. "Did you hear me? I'm sorry." His white hat lay crown down in the snow.

"For what?"

"Being a jackass and a jerk."

"Oh." She brushed snow off his shoulder. "Don't worry about it right now."

"I was thinking—if I laid down and slept like I wanted to, I'd never get to tell you I didn't mean it."

"You've got to get out of the snow." She got to her feet, took hold of his hand and pulled. "Come on, Jesse. Let's go inside."

"Can't." He resisted her tug. "Not that way."

As she watched, he rolled over to lie facedown in the snow. Then with the same slow-motion moves, he came up onto his hands and knees. From there, he pushed up until he knelt upright.

"Now, I need help."

Janie stood in front of him. Before anything else, she took off one of her gloves and wiped the snow from his face with her fingertips. "That's better. What next?"

But Jesse didn't say a word. He just knelt there in front of her, bareheaded, staring up into her face, his big blue eyes as serious and as intense as she'd ever seen them. Janie couldn't look away.

The next thing she knew, he was holding her bare hand in both of his. "Tell me you forgive me, Janie." Bending his head, he kissed her knuckles before looking at her again. "And then tell me that you'll marry me."

She couldn't believe what she'd heard. "Did you—"

The barn doors banged open behind her. Janie whirled to see Walker and Will striding out into the snow.

"Are you crazy?" Will was shaking his head.

As Jesse struggled to his feet, Walker put a shoulder underneath one arm, while Will supported the other. "You're risking frostbite out here, brother. This isn't the time for making snow angels."

Still looking at Janie, Jesse struggled to pull back. "Thanks, guys, but I'm busy. Let me go."

Walker shook his head. "We have orders from The Man."

"And The Woman," Will added. "We bring you inside or no Christmas dinner for us."

They dragged Jesse, still protesting, toward the barn. Janie followed. "I'll shut the doors," she called as they crossed the threshold.

"Thanks," Walker yelled.

"Janie—" Jesse started. Then the trio turned into the lounge doorway and whatever he wanted to say was lost.

Standing just where snowfall met concrete, Janie stared longingly into the Cody barn.

After a minute, though, she stiffened her backbone and pulled the sliding doors toward the center, first one, then the other, leaving herself on the outside.

By the time anybody realized she hadn't joined them—if they did—she'd be in her truck, speeding down the county highway.

Headed home, where she belonged.

Mark had been allowed to go home because Nicki would look after him. Jesse spent the night at his parents' house. He'd been too tired to argue with all of his siblings and their partners, too exhausted to insist on going home by himself. Janie had disappeared last night, without saying yes or no to either of his requests. So it didn't matter much where he went to bed.

He didn't wake up until J.W. knocked on the door and then walked in without waiting for an invitation. "You planning to sleep the day away?"

"I'm considering the option." Jesse propped his pillows on the headboard and leaned back against them. "I don't exactly feel like building a snowman this morning."

"Hands okay?" His dad sat down in a nearby armchair.

"Still tingling some." Jesse flexed his fingers. "No blisters, though. I do have a couple of blistered toes."

"Damn stupid thing to do, going out after that cow. We lose cows all the time."

Even J.W.'s bluntness couldn't get a rise out of him today. The effort just wasn't worth it. "We got the cow easy enough. It didn't seem right to leave a calf out there to die just before Christmas, if we could save it." He shrugged. "All's well that ends well. Right?"

His dad's keen brown gaze searched his face. "You don't look like you've reached any kind of happy ending."

Jesse shrugged. "I imagine you've talked to Mom."

"I have."

"I guess I should apologize—you aren't the only guilty party in this mess."

J.W. snorted. "Hell, son, nobody gets through this life guilt-free. We all make mistakes, all the time. Now, granted, some of those errors are more serious than others."

Jesse stared out the window into the backyard, where bright sunshine played over pine branches dolloped with snow. "Denying a boy the chance to know his father seems like a big one to me."

"Even back then, I didn't think Anne was unreasonable in what she asked. A man can't be faithful to two women—and their children—at the same time. If Abigail had let me see the boy, I would have had to choose eventually. Or else she would have had to let her son go. And I'm pretty sure she wouldn't do that."

"You're satisfied you did the right thing?"

The smile that split J.W.'s craggy face was almost tender. "How could I be otherwise? I've had four boys calling me Dad and growing up strong under the blue Wyoming sky. A little girl to spoil. A beautiful, passionate wife to share my days and nights. What more could I ask?"

The answer came from somewhere deep inside Jesse. "An NFR champion."

His dad laughed. "Yeah, that would have been good." Then he left the chair and came over to stand beside the bed. "But belt buckles and saddles and trophies don't make the ranch run, Jesse. I pushed all you boys to the limit with your rodeo skills, 'cause that kind of perseverance is what it takes to maintain an enterprise like ours. You take a fall, you get up and ride again. You make a decision that fails, you change your strategy and start again.

"All my sons are good men. But there's one lynchpin in this family, keeping everything together, making the machine run smooth. God knows I'm grateful, Jesse."

His dad's weathered hand came down onto Jesse's

shoulder. "You should know that, too. Now, more than ever."

Before Jesse could lift his own hand, another knock sounded on the door. J.W. went to open it.

"You're gonna spoil this boy," he warned his wife, who stood in the hallway with a tray of food. "He could get up and come downstairs to breakfast."

"Hush, John Walker. I can feed him anywhere in this house I want to." She set the tray on the table by the window. "I'm not going so far as to give you breakfast in bed," Anne said, looking all around the room to avoid making eye contact. "You can eat whatever you want and come downstairs when you're ready."

"I'm heading over to the barn," J.W. said from the doorway. "Be back for lunch." He didn't wait around for anyone to say goodbye.

Wiping her hands with a dish towel, Anne started to follow him. "Take your time. I'll just be—"

"Mom."

She halted in at the door, facing away from him.

"This is my week for apologies. You don't want to miss out."

He saw her shoulders shake with a brief laugh. "You had a right to be angry. I did something terrible."

"But I had no right to judge you." Jesse rubbed a hand over his face. "I've done too much of that lately. You should have reminded me about glass houses and casting stones."

His mother turned back and finally met his gaze. "Does that mean you'll be able to forgive me? I don't have any excuse, really…" She held up her hands in a helpless gesture.

Jesse slid out from underneath the covers and crossed the floor. "Your excuse is love. Love for Dad and for the family you wanted together. Starting with me." He cupped her elbows and drew her into a hug. "I guess I needed to grow up enough to admit that nobody's perfect." He felt her tears soaking into the shoulder of his T-shirt. "Not even you. But," he offered, hoping for a smile, "you're close enough."

"Thanks," she whispered.

He kissed her temple. "I love you, Mom."

"I love you, too." She straightened out of his arms, wiping her face with the dish towel. "Now, go eat something."

"Yes, ma'am."

"And, Jesse?"

"Mmm?" The food on that tray suddenly looked and smelled pretty good.

"Put some pants on before you come downstairs."

He glanced at his lap and realized he'd slept in just his underwear. "Will do."

THE MARKTON FEED STORE was closed on Christmas Eve. Most of the town's merchants, in fact, had stayed home. In honor of the season, their windows displayed decorations and lights, Christmas trees, elves and Santas and snow. Of course, they had more than enough of the real stuff outside. No spray flakes required.

With a half-price tree from Cody in the back of her truck, Janie rode slowly through town, hoping to dredge up some Christmas cheer. So far, the only thing she felt was cold.

Not for the first time, she decided to become more serious about attending church. Christmas was, at its heart, about believing in the miracles of grace and love that arrived on a long ago night with the birth of a baby. Markton offered several denominations to choose from, and she recognized the value of a faith-based community. Especially when you were losing a loved one.

But this year, she hadn't attended any worship services. Her mother wouldn't recognize Christmas from any other day of the year, and so Janie hadn't thought about trees or decorations or even a decent holiday dinner. Mark and Nicki would eat with her dad, or the Codys. Maybe both. Janie figured she would eat alone, as usual.

But today, with the sun-kissed world painted in white and blue and green like the interior of a snow globe, she'd decided she needed a Christmas tree. She would stand it outside and string it with all colors of twinkling lights. Surely that would lift her lonely spirits.

By the time the sun set, she had draped the tree with as many lights as it could hold. She even found a working extension cord and a socket to plug into. And she found herself smiling as she gazed at the cheerful blaze of color against the starry sky.

For the final step of her plan, she went into the house and ladled some warm spiced cider into a Christmas mug she'd bought for the purpose, also half-price. The sweet apple aroma filled the house and made even the undecorated rooms seem livelier. Carrying her cider, Janie went outside again and sat down on the front steps to gaze at her splendid tree.

"Merry Christmas," she said, raising her mug in a toast.

"Merry Christmas," someone replied.

She froze with the cup halfway to her mouth. "Jesse?"

He stepped out from behind the tree. "Hey, Janie."

"What are you doing out in the cold?"

"I didn't walk all the way from the ranch. Just the

corner." Coming closer, he nodded in the direction of town. "And I'm plenty warm. Ski gloves and liners, waterproof boots and two pairs of socks. Knit cap, which I hate."

"Learned your lesson, did you?"

"We miscalculated yesterday. Neither of us expected to spend much time outside on horseback. We would have dressed differently."

"I'm glad you're okay. Mark's good, too."

"Yeah, I talked to him earlier."

Such a casual remark for such a momentous event. "You two have…um…"

"Made peace?" Jesse chuckled. "Nothing so formal. But he offered his help yesterday, and I accepted. We'll move forward from there."

"Good. I think you can be friends, one day. You have a lot in common."

"Besides a father, you mean?" His question held no trace of bitterness that she could hear.

"Your love for the land and the animals. Your willingness to do the work."

"Not to mention a woman in our lives too stubborn to see how special she is. How much she matters."

Janie set her mug beside her on the steps and clasped her hands together on her knees. She didn't know what to say.

Jesse had come to stand right in front of her. "You ran away last night without giving me an answer."

Her laugh sounded hollow in the cold, still air. "Of course, I forgive you. You've been hit with some hard truths, lately—anyone would be stunned and confused. I just hope you've worked things out with your parents."

"We're family. That's what we do." He reached out

and took her hands in his, pulling her to stand up. "How about my second question?"

"I don't—"

"I can repeat it, if you want me to. Including the kneeling part."

"You shouldn't—"

But he was already on his knees in the snow. He'd removed his gloves at some point, and now he took hers off, too. His warm fingers fit in between hers, folding their palms together.

"I love you, Janie Hansen. I can't say when it happened—maybe that night you drove me home in the snow. Or maybe since we were teenagers, and I just never knew it."

"It doesn't matter," she told him. "I loved you then, enough for both of us. And nothing's changed."

Again, he kissed her hands, her fingers and wrists. "I want to marry you, Janie. You're the fire and the spice I need in my life."

She discovered she couldn't restrain her smile. "Stand up," she said, pulling on his hands. "Get out of the snow."

He got to his feet, then let go of her hands and pulled her into his arms. "Is that a yes?"

"I'll have to go away to school," she warned.

"Instead of riding bulls on the weekends, I'll make visiting you my personal rodeo." He attempted a wicked leer, which failed miserably.

"Your parents won't be too happy to have both Hansen kids in the Cody family."

"I suspect my parents have learned their own lessons the last few months."

She hesitated, head down, then said, "We have to take care of my mom."

Jesse lifted her chin with a finger. "It will be my honor to take care of your mother as long as necessary." With the same finger, he wiped away the tears on her cheeks. "Any other conditions?"

Janie pretended to consider.

He groaned. "You're killing me, here."

She put her hands on either side of his face. "Can we always be together for Christmas? And decorate a really big tree?"

"Till death us do part, I swear. Just say yes."

She released a breath she seemed to have been holding since she was fourteen years old. "Then, yes, Jesse Cody. I will marry you."

And with those words, their Christmas Eve turned quiet and reverent, just the way it always should be.

Chapter Fourteen

One year later

Jesse stepped into his parents' house and quietly closed the door behind him. He'd only left an hour ago, but the kid paraphernalia—miniature cars, dump trucks and fire engines, model horses and their tiny riders—scattered over the marble floor had disappeared. Thousands of white lights on the towering Christmas tree in the curve of the staircase twinkled as serenely as if this morning's predawn orgy of gift-opening and toy-tryouts had never occurred.

He found his brothers gathered in the living room.

"Here comes the groom," Walker said, raising a sippy cup in Jesse's direction before handing it to three-and-a-half-year-old Clay, standing between his knees. Father and son wore matching black jeans and dark green Western shirts. Leaning against the arm of Walker's chair was a stick horse name Silver, Clay's pride and joy this Christmas.

"That's a fine pony you got there," Jesse told the boy. "You put some miles on him this morning, didn't you?"

With the spout of the cup in his mouth, Clay gave him a big-eyed nod.

Dex sat by the window overlooking Cottonwood Creek, his still-healing leg propped on an ottoman. "Dusty's outside, trying to coax Matt away from Tinker for the wedding."

"Doesn't look likely." Jesse watched as the son his brothers shared brushed his new pony's black-and-white coat for what had to be the tenth time. "We might have to bring the pony into the house if we want Dusty and Matt at the ceremony."

"Mom will love that."

"Won't be the first time a horse found its way indoors on this ranch." J.W. came in from the kitchen, followed by Mark. "Which of you hellions was it that rode straight up the porch steps and through the front door, there at the old house?"

"Not me," Dex declared. "I'm the good twin."

Jesse socked him in the shoulder. "It most definitely was you, because Dusty was the one who dared you to do it. The hoof prints are still in the floor."

"You'll get your payback," J.W. said, sinking into his chair by the fire. From the healthy look of him, the past year of surgery and radiation treatments might never have happened. "Those twins of yours are terrors already. Never know where they'll be crawling to next."

"I caught Josh in the dog food bin this morning." Mark stood behind J.W., one arm propped on the mantel.

Jesse nodded. "Daniel had started up the stairs. You can't take your eyes off those boys for a second."

"Tell me about it." Dex wiped a hand over his face. "I'm thinking about chaining them in their cribs, so Josie and I can get some sleep."

Walker nodded, grinning. "Sleep. Right, that's what you're missing most."

"You would know," Dex fired back. "You're the one with the spitfire who's already walking at nine months."

"Yeah, but Terri falls asleep on my shoulder just like clockwork every night at nine. Unless she's sick, she doesn't wake up again till six."

"Which means," Will said, in a whisper everybody could hear, "that we'll have another baby around here in about…oh, nine months or so."

Walker only grinned.

"I'm the one who's sleepless." Mark gave what looked like an authentic yawn. "Five and a half months is hard work, let me tell you. Nicki's up every three hours."

Jesse cocked an eyebrow. "And you're the one who's sleepless?"

"Guilt."

"You're not kidding." Walker took the empty sippy cup from Clay and gave him a toy dump truck in its place. "I think there should be a support group on the internet for dads who feel guilty because their wives are the only ones who can soothe the baby."

"We can tell each other how hard we have it," Dex suggested.

"Commiserate on the way babies have changed our lives," Mark added.

"You don't know what change is," J.W. said with a grin, "until you've got three or four of them all running around at the same time."

Dusty and Matt had come in the back door just in time to hear the comment.

"Your mom's upstairs," he told his son. "She'll get you into the shower and show you what to wear." Then he looked around the room. "Pony's glad for some down-time, if you ask me."

"Not to mention you." His twin brother gave him a sympathetic grin.

Dusty, the World Champion Tie Down Roper for the year, dropped onto the couch. "The next hour's all yours, bro."

Dex nodded. "But not till after I get some of that wedding cake."

Jesse smiled as he buttoned the sleeves on his shirt cuffs. The minister should be arriving any minute now—the light dusting of snow that had fallen on the roads last night wouldn't postpone the ceremony. At exactly three o'clock on this sun-bright Christmas Day, he and Janie Hansen would get married. Finally, and forever.

Paula appeared in the doorway, looking beautiful in a dark green dress and carrying a dark-haired cherub with her mother's pansy-blue eyes. Seeing her dad, Terri immediately held out her arms.

"Dada," she said.

"I heard that." Walker grinned as he took the little girl into his arms. "Her first word."

"Of course." Paula stood on tiptoe to kiss her husband's cheek. "After all, who spoils her the most?"

The doorbell rang—"Home, home on the range…" Every adult in the room rolled their eyes.

Jesse watched as his dad leaned forward to stand up, but Mark put a hand on his shoulder. "Let me get it," he said quietly. The two men exchanged a look and Mark tightened his hold for a second, then went to answer the door.

A glance at the clock told Jesse that time had stopped. Still twenty minutes until the wedding. Would this afternoon last forever?

Will came to stand beside him. "Nerves?"

"Nope."

"You must be glad this day has finally come. I know I was."

Elly had spent the past year working toward another shot at the National Finals. This time, her training paid off with a big win and the title of World Champion Barrel Racer. She'd topped even that achievement, however, by getting married Vegas-style. She and Will and their families had attended the wedding chapel ceremony, complete with an Elvis impersonator singing "Love Me Tender." Afterward, the annual Cody bash had become a giant wedding reception.

That memory recalled to Jesse something he'd meant to say to his new brother-in-law. "We're grateful, by the way, to you and Elly for holding off your honeymoon till after today. Janie probably wouldn't marry me if she couldn't have my sister as her bridesmaid. It's been a law, I think, since they were twelve years old."

"No problem." Will put a hand on his shoulder. "Europe's not going anywhere, so this was the place we needed to be on Christmas Day."

Dusty stepped up beside them, now cleaned up and dressed in a fancy red shirt and good jeans. "My turn's next."

Will grinned. "Another one bites the dust?"

"Hell, no. I can't wait." Dusty looked toward the room's entrance. Maryanne and her dad had just arrived. Always dressed with style, today Dusty's fiancée wore a sophisticated and sexy blue dress that even Jesse could appreciate.

Dusty blew out a long breath. "Man, oh, man. She still takes my breath away. Talk to you boys later."

He stalked across the room and in front of everybody

including the minister, took Maryanne in his arms for a deep kiss. Even the whistles and catcalls from his brothers didn't break up the embrace until Dusty was good and ready.

Jesse fingered his bolo tie. Ten minutes. At this rate, he'd be an old man before he actually kissed his bride.

But all at once, everything started happening really fast. Josie appeared, carrying a little boy with blond hair and brown eyes—Josh. Right behind her, beautiful in an ice-blue dress, Anne entered with Daniel, the blue-eyed twin. Handing her armful to his father, she came straight to Jesse.

"You look so handsome." His mom patted his shoulders and straightened the tie he'd played with. Then she touched his cheeks with her fingertips. "Be happy, my son."

"I am." He bent to kiss her forehead. "Thanks for helping Janie this past year. You'll never know how much what you've done has meant to both of us."

Last spring, the severe decline in Abigail Hansen's health had required round-the-clock care and frequent hospital trips. Though dealing with J.W.'s illness and treatments, Anne had found the strength and time to visit Janie's mother, supervising her care and treatment in the nursing home and hospital to ensure Mrs. Hansen suffered as little as possible. Abby had passed away in September, peacefully and painlessly, with her children by her side.

Anne kissed his cheek, and let him go, without a reply.

"Let's take our places," the minister said. "Jesse, join me at the window, please."

Shrugging into his brown suit jacket, he took his

place beside the smiling clergyman. Mark and J.W. approached.

"See you boys again in a few minutes." Mark extended a hand. "Congratulations, brother." His other hand clasped Jesse's shoulder. "Glad to have you in the family."

Jesse duplicated the gesture. "Same here, brother."

J.W. took his place beside Jesse as his best man and offered a handshake in his turn. "You'll be a good husband," he said. "I know that and I'm proud of you."

Jesse gave his dad a hug. "I'm proud of you, too."

Finally, after what seemed like forever, Janie came down the staircase to stand beside him. She wore a lovely white dress and a cute white cowgirl hat with a short piece of lace like a veil in the back. Her beautiful dark eyes sparkled and her full red lips curved into a gorgeous smile as she repeated the words he'd waited a year to hear.

"I, Janie Hansen, take you, Jesse Cody, to be my lawfully wedded husband."

Then, at last, he got to kiss her.

Janie whooped at the top of her lungs when he picked her up high in his arms to whirl her around, laughing.

Their brothers and sisters and parents…the whole Cody family…laughed with them, and rejoiced.

* * * * *

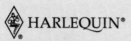

HARLEQUIN®

COMING NEXT MONTH

Available December 7, 2010

#1333 HER CHRISTMAS HERO
Babies & Bachelors USA
Linda Warren

#1334 A COWBOY UNDER THE MISTLETOE
Texas Legacies: The McCabes
Cathy Gillen Thacker

#1335 THE HOLIDAY TRIPLETS
Safe Harbor Medical
Jacqueline Diamond

#1336 THE BULL RIDER'S CHRISTMAS BABY
The Buckhorn Ranch
Laura Marie Altom

HARCNM1110

REQUEST YOUR FREE BOOKS!

2 FREE NOVELS PLUS 2 FREE GIFTS!

Love, Home & Happiness!

YES! Please send me 2 FREE Harlequin® American Romance® novels and my 2 FREE gifts (gifts are worth about $10). After receiving them, if I don't wish to receive any more books, I can return the shipping statement marked "cancel." If I don't cancel, I will receive 4 brand-new novels every month and be billed just $4.24 per book in the U.S. or $4.99 per book in Canada. That's a saving of at least 15% off the cover price! It's quite a bargain! Shipping and handling is just 50¢ per book.* I understand that accepting the 2 free books and gifts places me under no obligation to buy anything. I can always return a shipment and cancel at any time. Even if I never buy another book from Harlequin, the two free books and gifts are mine to keep forever.

154/354 HDN E5LG

Name	(PLEASE PRINT)

Address	Apt. #

City	State/Prov.	Zip/Postal Code

Signature (if under 18, a parent or guardian must sign)

Mail to the Harlequin Reader Service:
IN U.S.A.: P.O. Box 1867, Buffalo, NY 14240-1867
IN CANADA: P.O. Box 609, Fort Erie, Ontario L2A 5X3

Not valid for current subscribers to Harlequin® American Romance® books.

Want to try two free books from another line?
Call 1-800-873-8635 or visit www.morefreebooks.com.

* Terms and prices subject to change without notice. Prices do not include applicable taxes. N.Y. residents add applicable sales tax. Canadian residents will be charged applicable provincial taxes and GST. Offer not valid in Quebec. This offer is limited to one order per household. All orders subject to approval. Credit or debit balances in a customer's account(s) may be offset by any other outstanding balance owed by or to the customer. Please allow 4 to 6 weeks for delivery. Offer available while quantities last.

Your Privacy: Harlequin is committed to protecting your privacy. Our Privacy Policy is available online at www.eHarlequin.com or upon request from the Reader Service. From time to time we make our lists of customers available to reputable third parties who may have a product or service of interest to you. If you would prefer we not share your name and address, please check here. ☐

Help us get it right—We strive for accurate, respectful and relevant communications. To clarify or modify your communication preferences, visit us at www.ReaderService.com/consumerchoice.

HAR10R

HARLEQUIN®

A Romance

FOR EVERY MOOD™

Spotlight on

Classic

Quintessential, modern love stories that are romance at its finest.

See the next page
to enjoy a sneak peek from
the Harlequin® Romance series.

*See below for a sneak peek from our classic
Harlequin® Romance® line.*

Introducing DADDY BY CHRISTMAS by Patricia Thayer.

MIA caught sight of Jarrett when he walked into the open lobby. It was hard not to notice the man. In a charcoal business suit with a crisp white shirt and striped tie covered by a dark trench coat, he looked more Wall Street than small-town Colorado.

Mia couldn't blame him for keeping his distance. He was probably tired of taking care of her.

Besides, why would a man like Jarrett McKane be interested in her? Why would he want to take on a woman expecting a baby? Yet he'd done so many things for her. He'd been there when she'd needed him most. How could she not care about a man like that?

Heart pounding in her ears, she walked up behind him. Jarrett turned to face her. "Did you get enough sleep last night?"

"Yes, thanks to you," she said, wondering if he'd thought about their kiss. Her gaze went to his mouth, then she quickly glanced away. "And thank you for not bringing up my meltdown."

Jarrett couldn't stop looking at Mia. Blue was definitely her color, bringing out the richness of her eyes.

"What meltdown?" he said, trying hard to focus on what she was saying. "You were just exhausted from lack of sleep and worried about your baby."

He couldn't help remembering how, during the night, he'd kept going in to watch her sleep. How strange was that? "I hope you got enough rest."

She nodded. "Plenty. And you're a good neighbor for

coming to my rescue."

He tensed. Neighbor? *What neighbor kisses you like I did?* "That's me, just the full-service landlord," he said, trying to keep the sarcasm out of his voice. He started to leave, but she put her hand on his arm.

"Jarrett, what I meant was you went beyond helping me." Her eyes searched his face. "I've asked far too much of you."

"Did you hear me complain?"

She shook her head. "You should. I feel like I've taken advantage."

"Like I said, I haven't minded."

"And I'm grateful for everything…"

Grasping her hand on his arm, Jarrett leaned forward. The memory of last night's kiss had him aching for another. "I didn't do it for your gratitude, Mia."

Gorgeous tycoon Jarrett McKane has never believed in Christmas—but he can't help being drawn to soon-to-be-mom Mia Saunders! Christmases past were spent alone…and now Jarrett may just have a fairy-tale ending for all his Christmases future!

Available December 2010,
only from Harlequin® Romance®.

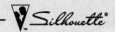

SPECIAL EDITION

USA TODAY BESTSELLING AUTHOR

MARIE FERRARELLA

BRINGS YOU ANOTHER
HEARTWARMING STORY FROM

When Lilli McCall disappeared on him
after he proposed, Kullen Manetti swore
never to fall in love again. Eight years later
Lilli is back in his life, threatening to break
down all the walls he's put up to
safeguard his heart.

UNWRAPPING
THE PLAYBOY

*Available December
wherever books are sold.*

Visit Silhouette Books at www.eHarlequin.com

SSE65566R

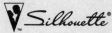

ROMANTIC
SUSPENSE

Sparked by Danger, Fueled by Passion.

RACHEL LEE

A Soldier's Redemption

When the Witness Protection Program fails at
keeping Cory Farland out of harm's way, ex-
marine Wade Kendrick steps in. As Cory's new
bodyguard, Wade has a plan for protecting her—
however falling in love was not part of his plan.

*Available in December
wherever books are sold.*